KIEV
FOOTPRINT

KIEV
FOOTPRINT

Carl A. Posey

DODD, MEAD & COMPANY   New York

To the Boulder Four with Love

1 2 3 4 5 6 7 8 9 10

Library of Congress Cataloging in Publication Data

Posey, Carl A.
    Kiev footprint.

    I. Title.
PS3566.O67K5   1983   813'.54   82-22186
ISBN 0-396-08115-0

Prologue

Vladimir Sergeevich Danilov shuts his eyes against the sudden claustrophobia that pursues and now overtakes him where he floats in the docking adapter of the American satellite, the membrane holding back the dark infinity of space. The pale, machined, curved walls speak of endless darknesses and stars and the brilliant curve of Earth beneath their orbit. His life-support system oppresses him, even in the weightless corridor between the two ships. He feels the mass, the volume, of his space suit and knows in his scrotum and stomach that, at some point on this journey, the silvered fabric will catch, suspend him; and he, afraid a freeing movement will split the pressure vessel that keeps him from exploding into the vacuum of space, will hang there eternally.

Ah, he thinks, this is only fear.

Unaccustomed fear.

One moment you're skipping along in your costume like a deep-sea diver, weightless in the sea. . . . The unbidden reference evokes Danilov as a pink and blond boy on the banks of the Kama, a tale of hard-helmet diving fresh upon his mind. It had come before, this sudden thrust of his childhood, the boy trying to claim the man. Yes, Danilov remembers now, it was an account of a fellow diver's suit tearing and the outside pressure cramming his entire body into his helmet.

One moment you're gliding like a diver, and the next, you're pushed into your hat.

He thinks, shoving the boy away: Mine is the opposite problem. And forces a grin upon his full lips. Perspiration still beads his plump, pink face, glistens on the blond eyebrows, salts the hooded, parrot-gray eyes, which he opens only with effort, driving the fear aside. He flicks on his torch.

Two meters ahead of him a white circle framed in the transparent horizon of his helmet marks the entrance to the airlock, through which he can enter the American ship. He floats head down in a vertical cylinder opened at the top like a metal flower, the adapter; and the adapter of his Soyuz, like some green, metal organ moves gently within this vertical receptacle, moves like the gunwale of a boat against a pier, for they are docked but unconnected, the two craft linked only by common velocity. For a moment Danilov wishes he had brought something to lash their adapter to the American ship's; then shakes his head, kicks toward the hatch, keeping himself centered in the hollow cylinder by deft touches of the metal walls. . . . Like a rower staying clear of rocks, as he himself, he remembers suddenly feeling the cold touch of his boyhood once again, as he himself kept his bark off the jetties at Cistopol. . . .

Ah, it was as though the boy who lived only in his memory wanted him dead today. I must get hold of things, he thinks. It is no time to go off on these rambles or to brood. Break your concentration and you die here. Remember that.

But misgivings fill his mind. He looks at the container he pulls behind him, too heavy to move on the ground; half his size, it follows him now like a tame grouper. He had been ordered to deliver this package, deliver it and unfurl its small antennae; and that was all. One smelled the KGB in it, a new odor at Zvezdney Gorodok when they trained for this flight, a new note in the ground controllers' voices. . . .

Voices. I could use a voice right now.

"Vladimir, are you all right?" As though responding to his thoughts, Yuriy Ivanovich Zhukov speaks on the intercom from the Soyuz above him. "Are you all right?" The voice comes to him guarded, almost a whisper.

"Yes, I'm fine," Danilov replies. Everything is fine, he thinks. In a technical sense, at least, the mission has been quite successful. Their Soyuz and a decoy had been fired spaceward like cannon rounds, pitched over into a flat trajectory that kept them down among the ghosts and angels and electronic ambiguities of the American radars that watched Soviet airspace. They had reached their target before they even crossed Tyuratam, when the controllers there had taken over the mission from Pleseck. Before they left Russia they had matched orbits and moved to within a few tens of meters of the American ship. The decoy had drifted out into a higher orbit, drawing American eyes away from the giant derelict he had now begun to board. Not everyone can achieve such an intercept, he thinks.

Really, a flawless mission—except for the damned adapter mechanisms. They had gambled here that the mechanisms would resemble those shown with the Shuttle replica at the Smithsonian Institution in Washington, which they had studied carefully and matched with their Soyuz adapter. And they had lost there, for the Shuttle adapter had been modified since *Columbia*'s early flight by the American reflex for change.

Danilov's pale eyes follow the torch beam over the bulkhead facing him. No gauges tell what the pressure is inside. Had the cabin and airlock lost pressure when whatever happened, happened? Or was the derelict's pressure compartment intact, with an atmosphere of pressurized air that, if he cracked the seal, would fire him like a torpedo back into the Soyuz? He smiles, thinking of the surprise his young commander would experience, having a fellow cosmonaut suddenly reappear—like the diver into his hat.

Well, intelligence had told them the hulk had zero pressure, although they had no way of knowing. Typical intelligence: when in doubt, manufacture. Danilov smiles. You're thinking like a virgin, he tells himself. You know all about intelligence. Except, he adds quickly, feeling the cold touch of a prayer gone sour, except I have tried to make things come right.

Danilov puts his free hand on the wheel that—how do the astronauts call it, that *dogs* the hatch shut?—and with something like a prayer upon his mind, and his body braced against the motion, turns it.

A faint breath of air issues into the adapter, or perhaps there is nothing at all. Without gravity one was always sensing tiny forces. The dark tunnel of the airlock yawns ahead of him. The sewerpipe, he thinks, of a greater city, as against this tiny one I'm in now, no larger than the drains we used to explore at Cistopol. Again, childhood plucks at him. He shakes his head to clear it of all revery. Gripping the rim of the hatch with his free hand, he pulls himself into the larger volume.

"Ah," he whispers, "ah." God, what had happened? The walls of the airlock are scorched, torn wiring waves like seagrass. At the base of the vertical cylinder, going off toward the crew section, the hatch has been smashed inward, as by a great, hot hand, and floats somewhere in the darkness beyond his light. What had happened? Intelligence had not given them *this*. And now, Danilov thinks, I know more than all of you about this grave. He shivers within his gleaming cocoon, floats down through the shattered airlock door into the larger volume of the crew quarters, pale walled, earth lighted, its views of stars and a crescent of Earth making space suddenly seem closer.

"Where are you now?" Zhukov whispers on the intercom.

"I have boarded," Danilov replies, a trifle annoyed. "Everything is fine."

He floats toward the ladder that will take him up through another hatch to the flight deck. Now there is enough Earthshine to show him the path of the burst of flame, of energy, that shattered the frail vessel and let in the vacuum of space. Yes, God, and *look*—vomit rattles in Danilov's throat; he turns away and then is forced to look at the floating body, a clothed skeleton whose skin has popped like an overinflated balloon's, whose blood and burst entrails drift in the room, rolled into the globules liquids become when weightless. Now he flies up through the hatch, where two other bodies, tied to their command and pilot seats, have exploded and now sit tethered, their skin floating like a diver's hair. They blur his mind, turn him toward housekeeping. The panel lights flash, run through their sequences, apparently unharmed . . . *unharmed!*

Danilov suddenly sees things clearly and shakes himself free of all the death. I knew it was a grave, didn't I? And isn't the game getting bloodier now? The instruments, everything but the pressurized cabin, are operating. I could call on the radio if I wanted. He laughs and says, "Houston, this is Cosmonaut Vladimir

Sergeevich Danilov aboard *Excalibur*." What a thing that would be. What a thing!

Almost contented, now, he bends to his work, clamping the container that has followed him beneath the payload operator's seat at the back of the cabin. He pushes the arming switch and extends two small antennae as far as they will go. And, when he has done his sapper's work, he thinks, there, they can do what they want now. They can play out their bloody game. "I'm finished," he says on the intercom.

"Good. We're forty minutes from the descent maneuver."

He starts back, flying once more, pausing at the entrance to the airlock, then says, "We have time, I want a quick look around."

"Yes, but hurry."

Danilov had been stunned as their Soyuz had overtaken the American ship, first by the beauty of having a ship of that size, so like an airplane, drifting in Earth orbit; and then by the complexity of its payload. The bays were open to space. Aft of the airlock and adapter, a large turret poked into the darkness, its head a nest of telescopes, large and small. Behind this, a folding arm held a relatively small ogival object some ten meters away and toward the rear of the Shuttle. He had been somewhat prepared for the unexpected—*Excalibur* had been the first seriously classified military Shuttle mission.

Now, moving aft beyond the airlock, following the scorched trail back to its source, he enters the turret, where another body floats, the last of *Excalibur*'s four-man crew. Danilov had believed the turret was a kind of broad-spectrum solar telescope and wanted to see it. Solar physics had been his specialty, and old Andreev his teacher. Without the seduction of flight, who knew where one might have gone? (Perhaps into bed with Andreev's daughter. They had come close, that time in Geneva. What we need is more romance and less intelligence. . . .)

"Yes, but this," he murmurs now, looking at the turret controls. Guessing, he thinks it has to be some sort of beam weapon or perhaps a high-energy laser. Looking toward the tail through a viewing port, he sees the peculiar package that seems almost to be held at arm's length from the spacecraft, a package painted red. . . . "No, glowing red. Glowing red," he whispers. A reactor, then, still running, perhaps overheating because no one is there to control it, pumping energy into the laser. "And all of this would have come down. All of this. While they gamble with each other, they bring this dirty bomb down on poor old Kiev."

But wait. *Wait.*

The ship had trembled, trembles now, like an aircraft in light turbulence. A ripple runs the length of its thin skin, vibrating through the deck into his cocoon. He peers through the station port. The Earth still moves steadily below, except that now it has a faintly eccentric turning motion too . . . yes, unmistakably, the big ship had begun to yaw gently back and forth, pivoting on the front end, swinging the docking station through an arc of perhaps ten meters. His added mass, or the impact of docking, or perhaps some new increment of drag from the high atmosphere—something had disturbed an already troubled orbit, stimulated this orbital death throe. In a moment, a day, a week, who knew how long, *Excalibur* would begin to cartwheel, and then the frictional hands of the atmosphere would pull it back to Earth.

Danilov's thoughts come clear as glass—as hard, as sharp—but encased in the fear of a dreaming man. He pushes away from the laser station, claws toward the adapter, and Soyuz. . . .

"*Vladimir!*"

Even as his name is shouted over the intercom he sees a crescent of light appear around the open hatch that expands until only the circular orifice remains, the stars shining beyond it.

"Vladimir, we've torn loose."

"Stay close, I'll come across the gap, just keep in close to the hatchway, please . . . " Danilov pants. He reaches the open hatch, forces himself to lean through. The American ship moves in a lazy arc, the adapter sweeping slowly past the Soyuz that holds its position just out of reach, a few meters from the path of the larger vessel but out of reach. "Yuriy," Danilov says in a voice he must reshape from a scream, "bring it in closer. I'll leap for it."

"Stay where you are. I'll try to dock."

The Soyuz carries no solar panels on this mission and looks like a pale, wingless insect that peers toward Danilov with a large, domed head. As he watches, the insect changes attitude slightly, flies a few meters to his right, then aligns itself to dock with a point in space.

Danilov shakes his head. Zhukov had lined up to dock as the larger vessel's adapter swung by. It was as futile as trying to thread a moving needle. The Soyuz drifts toward the swinging hatch now, and Danilov ducks back from the approaching spacecraft. He sees his colonel's face in the forward viewing port, a dark, Mongol face, looking all of twenty. *Excalibur*'s hatch swings to the right, inexorably, and seems to accelerate as the two vessels close. No sound comes from the collision, which catches the Soyuz on the docking adapter, spinning it like a bottle as it backs away.

"A close one," Danilov says.

"Yes, very close." The voice comes to him hurried, a little frightened; then silence as the Soyuz is brought under control, its flat spin damped out with the thrusters. "I'm going to try again."

The Soyuz repeats the maneuver, positioning itself to dock with a future point on the arc described by the Shuttle's docking port. Again it approaches the hatch as the big ship swings to meet it. For an instant the adapter thrusts into the docking port; but it stays only for a moment before the larger ship's movement ejects it. Danilov, in his ungainly suit, cannot move swiftly enough to reach the Soyuz.

"Once more," says Zhukov.

"Once more," Danilov echoes hopelessly.

The Soyuz pushes itself back into an angled docking position and heads in. The American ship's docking port swings toward the approaching adapter. Danilov's hopes rise. But again, the bigger ship brushes the Soyuz aside, sends it spinning. The colonel is silent until he has his capsule back under control. Then, "Vladimir, we are coming up on our last descending node. In the next minute or so Tyuratam will bring the decoy back this way and put me on automatic control. Then they will begin the descent maneuver." Zhukov's voice trembles with emotion, surprising Danilov and calming him.

"Bring it as close as you can. I'll try to get across."

"You can't do that. It's out of the question."

"Would you leave me here?"

"I'll try, then." The Soyuz creeps forward, taking up a station only two meters from the docking port of the American ship. Danilov pushes through the hatch as far as he can without letting go and stretches his free hand toward the approaching adapter. His fingertips swing by only a meter away from the smaller craft, and he tenses his muscles to leap the gap.

But he cannot force himself to fly untethered across open space. His mind is his enemy today, and fills with possible trajectories, leaps that will take him past the gray hull of the Soyuz, his fingers just brushing it, and then the long, circling fall back to Earth, the fiery return to the atmosphere. . .

"I can't," he says.

"I don't blame you," Zhukov responds.

"Can you tell Tyuratam our situation?"

"You know our orders."

"Of course."

"I wish there were something to be done."

"God knows you tried to help me, comrade."

"Yes, God knows." A moment later, Zhukov says, "There . . . Tyuratam has taken control of the spacecraft. They are bringing us . . . me . . . back in. I'm sorry. Good-bye."

"Good-bye," Danilov replies, and makes a friendly salute to the dim figure behind the viewing port.

Retrorockets on the Soyuz flicker, and the spacecraft drops suddenly, swiftly away from the American ship. Danilov watches it go, watches it become a gray speck and then disappear against the distant canopy of clouds.

He still leans through the hatch, half inclined to throw himself to Earth after all. Earth . . . and more than Earth . . . *Russia* moves beneath his orbit now. The Soyuz had braked when they turned to the descending node of their orbit, over the Gulf of Finland, all shrouded by clothlike bands of clouds curving southward from the Barents Sea. He watches the weather above his homeland wheel past. Then, east of Moscow, the clouds part, and he sees the river-laced lowlands and, yes, the distinctive sky-colored Y where waters from the Kama and the Vantka conflow with the Volga. Cistopol would be at the top of the right arm of the Y. Cistopol, where he had been a boy. Ah, God, that is the place whose memory he could not shake today, the place of his boyhood, when he had lived along great rivers, dreaming of diving, dreaming of flight. . .

Nothing would make him leap to Earth above his very cottage, the graves of his parents, the fields of his friends. He watches the *Y* of water out of sight, watches Russia until she ends among the hard, sandy mountains to the southeast. Then he seals the hatch and floats back toward the death-filled flight deck of *Excalibur*, the grave, prepared to die.

PART ONE

"How come an agency like NASA, which measures every contingency down to a gnat's testicle, with the *Skylab* experience behind it, would overlook the rather glaring possibility that a hundred-ton spacecraft wouldn't burn up on reentry?"

"In a word, Steve, we fucked up."

1

Vlad Danilov was on my mind when the whole thing began for me, and I guess he will be until it ends, if it ever does. I heard about him on the car radio, the fifty-word wire-service story dropping the sudden news of a friend's death into the cheery brilliance that hovers over Biscayne Bay on any summer afternoon. I was on my way out to Key Biscayne to cover an Astrogeophysical Union conference, to hear scientists talk about the heavens; and now the sky was full of death. For we were in those days of restless national mourning over the astronauts still aboard the shuttle *Excalibur*. That day, Dan Rather would end his newscast with "That's the news, on this thirty-fifth day of silence from space shuttle *Excalibur*." You remember how it was, of course; all of us wore at least a figurative black armband for the lost astronauts, for White and Hess and Frisch and Carroll, and many of us wore a real one, like the yellow ribbons people used to wear for the hostages in Iran. Except that White, Hess, Frisch, and Carroll were hostaged to some unknown accident that silenced *Excalibur* one night on the far side of the world, something sudden and unexpected, one of those "impossible" accidents that seem to happen all the time with spacecraft and oil platforms and reactors. A few days later, we heard NASA believed they were dead, that the accident had destroyed all ability to bring the ship back in a computer-controlled reentry and landing and that another Shuttle mission was being mounted as speedily as possible to recover their bodies and examine the crippled spacecraft. But the aging *Columbia* had resisted all efforts to ready her for flight, losing tiles, regurgitating fuel, reluctant perhaps to fly into the great graveyard of space. They knew only what their giant telescopes could tell them: *Excalibur* flew upright with respect to earth, no visible signs of damage, in a low and steadily decaying orbit, silent as a tomb.

And I heard the Danilov report amid violence of the ordinary, random, terrestrial kind: I'd stopped in a line of cars that crept by a bad head-on farther out the causeway, the bloody tangle and blanketed forms spread around a lane and a half, the rest of us going by like mobile mourners. So news of Danilov, right from the start, evoked smashed machines and covered bodies vibrating under Florida's harsh summer sun. And all the death to follow began with death, death after death in space, death spread around the causeway.

The radio voice quoted Tass to the effect that Danilov had been killed during a Soyuz reentry malfunction. His command pilot had "miraculously escaped." No details were available on the nature of the malfunction, but our Air Force confirmed that the Soyuz had "separated structurally" prior to reentry. And on, the story faintly tainted, for governments never simply tell the truth. But at the time I wanted to remember the dead, not search for reality in a Soviet release. If asked, I would have said his death marked the end of something, not the beginning.

It took awhile for me to pull Vlad into focus, like bringing a body up from the bay—you saw the face down through the blue, deformed by turbidity and optical pranks, not terribly recognizable; and then, closer to the surface, the person came clear. By the time I drove by Planet Ocean, the rubber band of traffic I was in had expanded a little, and Danilov had appeared in my memory, a stocky frame in the Soviet dark blue suit, crisp, oiled, bowl-cut blond hair, the pudgy face of a Russian boy, the boy-grin as the face came to life, framing gray grown-up eyes. I spent the rest of the drive out to the Rosenstiel School remembering the brief, cheerful encounter from which we'd drawn a kind of friendship and his occasional awkward, oddly worded notes.

On my way into the plush, paneled hall where the Astrogeophysical Union had assembled all those people to talk about their science, I was intercepted by Randy Jones, a big, hard-eyed woman from Santa Fe who handled media for the AU, and a friend, of sorts, of long standing. "Remember Vlad?" she asked.

"Heard about him on the radio."

"Nice man." Her eyes sparkled, like the granite eyes of a fat statue starting to cry.

"Very." Then, to steer us away from death, I asked, "Anything up this afternoon?"

"Sonya Van Deer's giving a press briefing on the new sunspot cycle. You might like that one. It'll be after her paper."

"Good."

"Thanks for coming out, Steve."

"It's just possible one of those excited oxygens will molest a hydrogen and give us a story."

"Sure." But it made her laugh, so that a girl appeared in the pale, pitted oval of her face. Somewhere, not very long ago, she'd been somebody's daughter. Then the girl vanished and the hard, dykey look recaptured Randy.

I was late getting to a seat about halfway down the auditorium aisle, causing a Brazilian, or perhaps a German, to interrupt his incomprehensible discussion of ions in the thermosphere and frown at me. Once installed, I listened to another paragraph or two, then crossed him off my copy of the agenda, tuned him out, and thought about Danilov some more.

Earlier I said we'd shared a kind of friendship. Maybe it wasn't even that. We'd spent only a long afternoon together, once, at the Cape, back in the Apollo–Soyuz days. In a way this story began there, although none of us felt then the imperceptible folding of events across our lives, linking us.

I'd been out with the cosmonauts and other journalists, herded from display to display by the NASA PR people, through the drowning heat and humidity of that mid-Florida spring. Finally I gave it up and went back to the administration building press room, a green-walled place that, like the rest of the Space Center facilities, had begun to look a trifle worn. I came in on Randy, who did NASA public information then, and John Chester, an agency engineer who wore a bow tie beneath his thin, elliptical, faintly equine face and, in the middle of the 1970s, still knew where to get his copper-colored hair crew cut, and did. In fact, while you knew he had sprung from the copulation of humans, endured a childhood, been schooled, and all the other things we must do to become adults and make a living, he seemed to have come from nowhere but the 1950s. He was an empty man to me, almost faceless, almost lifeless, without emotion except that his voice carried a mincing sound that made it easy to imagine John holding a younger man's hand in a dim bar. As Randy evoked a vanished, loving father, Chester evoked the possibility of a large, evacuated eggshell somewhere, and no one, and nothing.

My first impression of them had been that I'd surprised them together; if they'd been in bed their expressions would have fit. But then the surprise cleared from their eyes as quickly as from actors', and they welcomed me in and kidded me about mad dogs, Englishmen, and Canaveral's noonday sun. Then we turned inward, Randy working on an agenda, Chester daydreaming, I supposed, about what engineers daydream about, and I trying to shake the bullshit out of my notes.

The door opened and one of the second- or third-crew cosmonauts, lumpily Russian in a navy blue suit, half-entered before he noticed us. "Oh, sorry," he said in a thin, athlete's voice and good accent.

"No, come in, Captain Danilov," Randy said quickly, coming to her feet with surprising lightness; she was both lighter and prettier back then. "You know Mr. Chester," and the cosmonaut nodded. "And this is Steven Borg, a journalist."

"Vladimir Sergeevich Danilov," he said as we shook hands.

"Nice to know you," I said.

For a moment we stood around in silence, and then Danilov said, "I didn't mean to intrude. I was looking for . . . a place for eating."

"The cafeteria?" Randy asked.

"Yes, exactly, the cafeteria."

And I, following timeless instincts toward a less-structured interview, said, "Look, why don't we get lunch outside?"

He almost shook his head. Then, seeing nothing but good humor from the three of us, he grinned like a boy and nodded. "I would like that."

"Will they let you out?" I asked.

"Oh, they don't seem to mind, since I have a little English."

So the four of us got into my rented Malibu and drove into Cocoa and had martinis and seafood in a waterside place where the waitresses wore almost as much as the shrimp, and we talked about everything except Apollo–Soyuz. More of a philosophical quest, that afternoon, and my memory of it on this first day of trying to get it back was not too crisp.

I remembered that Randy got a little tipsy and laughed a lot and that Chester went quiet on us, watched the sea, although he had an occasional hand in the conversation; he seemed to steer. Mainly I remembered that Vlad and I drank and ate and talked about our boyhoods and compared them a little, his growing up along his rivers, my growing up on mine (the Mississippi and the Ohio). We talked floods and harvests and rowboats and canoes, women, how we looked at science from our separate perspectives, how he got out of solar astronomy, how I got out of English lit, our fathers . . .

God, we talked about everything.

Somewhere in the middle of all this, I remembered then, lay a funless spot, a kind of black hole in the midst of good humor. It had come when Danilov and I got around to civil liberties—an American talking to a Russian about civil liberties has the same purchase on the material as a black talking to a white on the same subject and is as easily annoying. I'd bitched about the level of personal freedom in the Soviet Union. He'd sneered or done a polite, apple-cheeked imitation of a sneer. And said what? I swam back through the martinis, trying to remember. A flushed Russian boyface, a moment's anger. But what the hell had he said? It wouldn't come, at least not then.

Anyway, we got Vlad, as we had come to call him, back to NASA near ten that night, returned as drunk and comradely as two new roommates at a university, and the three of us delivered up the one of him to a couple of NASA cops and a Russian I supposed was his commissar.

We never saw one another again, but we kept in loose touch. Now and then a letter would come from Danilov when he traveled out of Russia. I sent notes with Christmas cards. Once he called collect from a pay phone in New York, just to talk, he said; and we had. So we had fragments between us. But on that first afternoon of his death I saw mainly that I had a bunch of memories to unpack and inventory, by way of laying Vlad to rest.

I worried the morning after our one encounter, after I was sure of surviving my hangover and had almost stopped sweating pure gin, that we had crippled his career, taking him out that way. I guess I even thought fleetingly that we had somehow pointed him toward death that afternoon. And so we had, but not in the way I meant, or in any way I understood on the day we heard our friend had joined the other dead in space.

But my main regret, one that is still pretty new with me, is that I accepted the party, the friendship, the encounter as a gift, without skepticism, and didn't see until way too late that more had gone down at that restaurant in Cocoa than a gross of martinis and shrimps. For it was on that day, I began to believe later, that Danilov decided to cancel what he must have considered a fatal wrong turn and that a friendship with me could help him do it.

2

Sonya Van Deer's paper was the last of the afternoon, and rescued me and the other reporters there from all the boredom of the day's interminable (and unimportant) series of papers. She had something to say: Using a technique developed by the Russian Andreev, she derived a prediction of solar flare activity for the coming cycle that was much higher than had been predicted by NASA thus far. The message translated into prose; a story might be filed.

But, for me, she was something beautiful seen at the right instant—the lovely violinist one picks out of the orchestra, the fall of hair, the face entranced and somnolent against the rich wood of the instrument, the rhythmic motion of shoulder, arm, and bow, all seen from the back of a hall, the subject hardly larger than a fingernail. The beautiful Dr. Van Deer.

Randy Jones had promised her to us after the session, so we waited in a platoon of beige metal chairs ranked at one end of the press room. I sprawled in a middle row, a long arm securing my trunk in one chair, a long leg anchoring me to another, conscious of trying to be something as yet undefined, but not necessarily a skinny writer in his thirties, who'd let his hair grow and wore a sand-colored suit cut along the lines of a spinnaker. I wanted Sonya Van Deer to see me. The pose made me jumpy, and I looked around for colleagues and competitors. Williams, who wrote weather and occasional science for the afternoon paper, was there, pale and callow as a Victorian boy. Nelson had come over from

AP, and I saw that the interplanetary fare of the day frightened him: He'd expected to understand a word, a phrase, here and there, but the meeting had passed in a dream of tongues. Pomerance, the *Newsweek* stringer, had come, probably because his wife had some task connected with the conference, and Dewey Jones, who wrote for *Aviation Week,* was there in his chocolate leisure suit and aviator glasses, an older man whose hair lengthened, whose clothes became more dashing as he aged. Another nod of recognition.

The others were just faces, young and Cuban, nervous and girlish, broadcasterish and stupid; except one, a block of a man in his forties with the eyes of a bad cop, the deep glare of a grizzly, wearing a blue blazer and gray slacks, like a bear dressed as a realtor. He returned my look as calmly as an animal, then smiled with yellow teeth, forcing an involuntary nod from me. I thought he must be there as a shill, except, since this press conference lacked a point of view, who needed one? The sun? I smiled privately and put the stranger down as a public-affairs type from Van Deer's agency.

She entered then, and the attention of the small group shifted toward her. At close range, Sonya Van Deer was less delicate, less the distant face and gleam of polished wood of the orchestral vision; and older, maybe forty. The tanned ellipse of her face enclosed pale eyes and a full, unlipsticked mouth. Her blond hair stretched back into a gold rope that descended nearly to her waist in the back—a braid, I decided, I must unweave. She wore a severely cut pants suit of gray silk, beneath which her athletic body moved visibly, freely. As a very young man I'd had a girl friend who liked to challenge me with, "I can still take your breath away." Maybe she could and maybe she couldn't. Sonya Van Deer definitely could. Except . . . as she surveyed the small audience there assembled, her glance swept me without a pause; nothing passed between us. It hurt, for I was radiating at peak power.

"My name is Sonya Van Deer," she said in a clear voice faintly touched with Europe. "I really have nothing to add to my paper, but if you have questions I'll try to answer them."

Sensing a question forming behind me, I brought myself out of my sprawl and reconnoitered quickly. Grizzly eyes had his hand up like an outsized student, a definite agency plant I decided. So I got up and began to talk before my questions were quite formulated.

"Dr. Van Deer, I'm Steve Borg from the *Herald*." She turned a look on me that said, You're not the reporter I need right now. I looked back unblinkingly, hoping to project this counterthought: I want to undo your braid. And tried to think of a reasonable question. What was her subject? And, uh, who cared? "Your, uh, prediction of higher sunspot numbers . . . of more flares on the sun during this new cycle than others have predicted . . . what does that mean to the, uh, woman on the street?" A little humor. I leered.

"Well, Mr. Borg, it can mean quite a lot to people of all sexes." Laughter. She gave a cold smile, continued. "A flaring sun presents a radiation hazard to manned space flights and to passengers aboard high-altitude jet flights in polar regions. It means some brownouts and blackouts perhaps, fades in radio and long-line communications. Some satellites are affected in adverse ways, as are over-the-horizon radars that use the ionosphere as a reflecting layer. CB radios will experience more fades from bursts of radio noise from the sun. But then the ionosphere will be denser as a result of greater ionization from solar activity, so that they should also get more range."

The competition still shuffled behind me; so I pressed on, wanting to keep myself before this lovely woman until she rewarded me with more than a fishy gray eye. "So an active sun would actually heat up the upper atmosphere and cause it to expand?"

"That's correct."

It had been a dandy scientific question, and it brought some blood into the discussion. I am not a dummy, goddamn it! was my new thought for projection. My colleagues should be packing their bags about now. "Wouldn't that also affect satellite orbits?"

She flushed. "Yes, I forgot to mention that. Spacecraft in low orbits would experience more atmospheric drag. It would tend to shorten their orbits."

"So, a more active solar cycle would begin to bring back some of the low orbiters?"

"It could contribute."

I flipped through such mental files as I had of satellites in low orbits and quickly came to the big one. "Like *Excalibur?*"

"*Excalibur. . .*" I watched her think her way through a short silence, excited that I'd opened a door she felt she must enter carefully. She threw a look almost of longing across the group, and I followed it to her bear, who nodded almost imperceptibly, without moving his head, like a prisoner talking in the yard. Something in her face did the work of a shrug, and she said to me, as though no one else was in the room, "The shuttle's orbit has been decaying for some time. I think this is generally known. If we estimate the rate of decay based on low sunspot numbers, we can say the vehicle will reenter late next year. If we use a very high sunspot number—such as the number I reported today—the reentry would come much sooner."

"How much sooner?"

"A few months perhaps. I can't say."

"How do you feel about your prediction?"

"I'm very confident that Professor Andreev's technique is correct. I've used it to calculate sunspot numbers for past solar cycles, and it has been very close to the mark each time."

There'd been something on the wire about an *Excalibur* rescue mission. I pressed on. "So what you're saying is that NASA can't get another shuttle up to *Excalibur* in time to make a controlled reentry or boost it to a higher orbit?"

"I don't like to speak for another agency. But, yes, that's how things look."

Something was still missing. I tried to come quickly to what was wrong with this picture. "But all that really means is a derelict satellite will burn up in the atmosphere, doesn't it? Another Skylab."

"*Excalibur* is a very big derelict, Mr. Borg, and there are those thousands of ceramic tiles to keep it from burning up on reentry. But," and she half-shrugged again, "this is really off my subject, and I hope you'll check with NASA on these points."

"Does NASA know about your predictions?"

"We've forwarded them to the *Excalibur* people at Huntsville."

"And they still want to try a rescue mission?"

"I can't speak for them, Mr. Borg. They have a very expensive shuttle mission under way to rescue *Excalibur*. It may be that they are reluctant to give it up."

Okay, I thought, now you'll remember me. "Thank you, Dr. Van Deer." I sat down. A couple of the others asked their questions, which, incredibly, took the conference away from the start I'd made, pointing it more toward the effects on citizen's band radios. I looked back to see how police eyes had taken my performance and found the big man gone. So I went over to Randy, in the back of the room, and asked, "Who was the guy who left?"

"I dunno," she replied.

"Not press?"

"Not hardly. I thought he came from Sonya's agency, but it turns out not." She examined some cards. "He signed in as Andre Cerf, from 'International Earth-Space Enterprises.'"

"Whatever that is."

"You doing a story, Steve?"

"Oh, sure."

"Breaking the silence in the press about our meeting."

"It's a hard one to cover."

"You mean only science writers like you can understand it."

"Of course," and we both laughed.

I turned back to the interviews. Williams doggedly pursued the matter of increased range for CB operators. Nelson had already got up to go, satisfied he could squeeze a twenty-line wire-service piece out of what he had and beat everyone with it. I focused once more on Sonya Van Deer, regretting that this would be all we had together: The braid would leave Miami, and I would not have had a chance to unweave it. She was talking to Williams but looking beyond him, I thought at first, for her bear. But her gray eyes continued to sweep the room after they found him gone, until they came to me, and for a moment we stared at one another, and there was an exchange. Not hostility, not that exactly. But nothing especially friendly, either. Maybe I'd just made an impression that told her I was a shit. "So it goes," I muttered.

Still, I hung around, and when she finished her response to Williams's questions she said she thought that would be all today and thanks very much. Her voice had a strained note in it, as though something had gone wrong. I stalked her as she made for the door, as she began to hurry. "Dr. Van Deer, wait . . ." She ducked toward the exit and I caught her arm, a tough arm at that, and said, "No, come on . . ."

She whirled at me. "For God's sake, Mr. . . . Borg, let me pass."

"Just . . . wait a minute. I wanted to ask you . . ." God, her face could get hard. "I'd like to pursue some of the questions a little further. Could we do it over dinner tonight?"

"Ah, Mr. Borg," and she laughed, seemed to relax. I wasn't the devil, just a libidinous young male. "Thank you for the invitation, but I really can't."

"Really?"

"Really."

"I'm disappointed."

"You may not believe this, Mr. Borg, but so am I, a little."

"Okay," and I laughed for her. "A little disappointment goes a long way with me."

"Yes, I felt it would." She echoed my laugh; the sound made me want to hear it in a forest, with my eyes shut, my head in the lap of the body that bore the braid, that . . . "Good-bye," she said and went past me out the door. Out of my life, I supposed.

Randy Jones waddled over, walking on legs so heavy she had to move them laterally to get them past each other. "No score tonight, Steve."

"I really had dinner in mind."

"Yeah, I saw you calculating the beef, old sport."

"Where's she from, Randy?"

"Alamo Peak Observatory."

"No, I mean originally."

"Switzerland, I think."

"Think the paper'd pay a research trip to Alamo Peak?"

"Maybe Sonya really doesn't want to see you."

Something proprietary in her voice made me mad. "She gay?"

A look I'd seen before swept her face, something between tears and a war mask, as she decided whether to crumple or grab me by the throat. But she said, "You don't fight fair, Steve."

"Sorry. You looked like a picador to me."

"Then I'm sorry too."

"Okay. So what did you mean?"

"I just find something . . . I didn't really buy the way she gave her paper, she seemed kind of wired or something."

"Explain."

"Can't. Just some vague odor, you know?"

I knew. Sonya Van Deer had responded to me as though I'd intruded, when, obvious attraction notwithstanding, I was really just a reporter squeezing out a story. I'd interrupted something. But what? Who'd want to channel a story about the frigging sun? I shook my head and cleared it of everything but Sonya and the braid. "Be that as it may, Randy, I think she'll be seeing me again."

"If you get out to Alamo Peak, you can stay at my place. Santa Fe's only a couple hundred miles away."

"I'd like that."

"Me too."

"I'll try. Now, best I go file something."

"You taking the shuttle or CB angle?"

"Shuttle, natcherly. Be plenty of CB stories without one from me." I patted her bicep. "Take care, Randy. See you in Santa Fe."

"I hope you do, Steve." Her voice came to me girlish and friendly; it didn't square with all the hard unhappiness I saw in her face. That unhappy look haunts me. It appears on my mental horizon spontaneously, uninvited, and forces me to look at it and to think of what happened out in that red- and copper-colored desert. In these encounters I've come to see it as proof of Randy's friendship. Even that early she knew how it all must go and worried about me—no, I should say, regretted me.

3

Consider this: One morning the people of the world are told of a great sword of Damocles swinging in the sky above them, a sword that, in a week, a year, will make its lethal descent, biting into the earth along a thousand-mile corridor. News of this eventuality, one thinks, brings panic, returns to God, philosophical stirrings, lamentations, and rendings of garments on the grand scale. And one is wrong. The *Skylab* experience—a gentle rain of tin over empty Australia—had greatly dulled the edge of old Damocles' sword. So the tale of the flying sword sputters for a few days before being replaced by countertales of what the government is doing about it. The epic becomes just another installment in the serial we call the news. No one much cares when the story breaks or misses it when it is gone.

That was how the *Excalibur* reentry story broke. I wrote a piece that night about how a highly active sun could bring the derelict shuttle down long before its managers expected, before a *Columbia* mission could boost it to a higher orbit or drive it into the sea; about how a hundred tons of metal and synthetics, refractories, and fibers would lose the critical increment of velocity; how friction and the shock of hitting the denser atmosphere would cause the big vehicle to shatter and glow white hot, but that much of it would come back in this projectile, and bits of this, bits of that, would shower the Earth and its people. No one would know where the reentry point would be until perhaps a day, perhaps only a few hours, before the derelict started in. At NASA they

called the reentry corridor a footprint, a term I liked for its suggestion of a great sandaled foot descending from the sky. But when I
gave my clarion call of alarm, no one seemed to give a shit. Better
to write ball scores.

Oh, it became a pretty big story much later, closer to the event,
when NORAD began issuing its *Excalibur* reentry countdown (so
many more days of orbit, this projected footprint) and the media
began to cluster on the reentry itself. But at the beginning, things
were slim. The AP ran something blending the shuttle story into
something on solar activity and skips in CB radio transmissions.
My piece ran the next morning in the *Herald*, which, for the
record (in case someone keeps track of such things), broke the
Excalibur reentry story. And, for a time, that was it. Then we
began to see a little here, a little there, nothing very comprehensive
until Browne's piece in *Discover*; then a few ripples of interest,
something in *Science*, then silence. And then a rash of NASA press
releases on what NASA scientists were doing about the problem,
trying to regain control of the big ship, losing it, and on, as the PR
people began saturating the system, deftly seizing control of the
story.

It wasn't science journalism's finest moment. But then I'm in a
business where people like to think of themselves as incapable of
understanding anything technical. If you don't, your editor may
treat you like editors used to treat college grads. And while it is
true that many reporters can't write about longitude and latitude
without screwing them up, I think the nontechnical thing is mainly
a pose, a shuffling humility put on so they can share the brain-
smoothing simplicity they assign to their readers. Well, some
readers are and some readers aren't. But you can destroy a lot of
skill, writing to all that supposed simplicity. If my nontechnical
colleagues acted that stupid about city hall or the school board,
they'd have their asses fired.

On that day of learning Vlad Danilov was dead, of meeting
Sonya Van Deer, of hearing about *Excalibur* and the sun—on that
May Wednesday I got back from Virginia Key about five-thirty
and parked the yellow bug out front. I then entered the great glass
wall, said hello to Murray, the old boxer who passed for a guard,
and took the elevator up to my floor. The city room had lost the

tension it had around the first deadline at three-thirty and was beginning to tense up for the next one, in the ebbing and flowing activity from which one of the better newspapers in the country sprang, a miracle, each morning. At this time of day almost everybody was there, but almost no one was as busy as in the early afternoon, so that there was a tendency to bullshit out where we reporters sat, not quite able to see the Atlantic through the executive offices lining our eastern wall. I crouched in my twenty or so square feet of the city room and called Les Dunham.

He'd been a science-writing colleague who'd floated up pretty high in civil service by way of a speech-writing job on a presidential science advisory board and had now about reached his level of incompetence way up in the NASA public-affairs structure. I got Dunham before he fled to the suburbs, his abrasive Boston voice bringing dismay wherever it was heard, bringing it to me as he came on the line. It evoked the mean, weary little man. "Hi, Les," I told the dismaying voice. "Steve Borg in Miami."

"Oh, sure. Hello, Steve." His tone told nothing; of course I wondered why.

"Got a minute?"

"Sure."

"Good. Look, I'm working on a shuttle story and need some help."

"What kind of shuttle story, Steve?" He had that guarded sound that meant, Tell me what you know and I'll try to keep this thing contained. Again, I wondered why.

I told him about Sonya Van Deer's paper that afternoon, the briefing, and what we had come to about *Excalibur*'s reentry. Perhaps I heard some intake of breath, or maybe it was just the wire sighing between Miami and D.C. "I guess what I need, Les, is a better idea of what's going to come back in. The odds of being hit. The amount of warning time. That kind of thing."

"I'm not sure I'm the right guy. I'm glad to help out, but you might get better stuff from the Huntsville public-affairs shop."

"I doubt it. I won't quote Les Dunham."

"Fair enough." A pause while he figured out how he was going to walk me through this mine field, then, "The first thing I'd stress is that nobody really knows what will survive the reentry and what won't. Then I'd stress the fact that I'm not technically up to speed on the problem. I mean, I don't know what our technical people are thinking."

"Okay," I said, remembering that Les had always kept his own technical prowess pretty well concealed as a reporter but that his degree was in physics.

"Maybe the whole structure will come back intact. Maybe it'll get wrenched and bent up and still come back in as a recognizable lump plus a bunch of little fragments. My guess is it'll fly on in and crash somewhere—but this isn't the sky falling, Steve. It's just an airplane crash."

"Where?"

"Nobody knows."

"You can't predict the reentry?"

"Nobody can, not until it's right around the corner."

"How big an area will it cover?"

"The word here is a thousand-mile footprint."

"Footprint. God."

"Just our way with words, Steve."

"Sure. Now, what about the difference in sunspot numbers? I mean, NASA's been looking at values under a hundred, while Sonya Van Deer's up nearly twice that."

"Right, and some people in another corner of Van Deer's own agency are looking at values maybe halfway in-between. This isn't science; it's fucking art. You get a lot of differences. We thought our numbers were okay. Maybe they weren't. But then again, maybe they are."

"Any chance NASA'll get up to boost it higher or anything?"

"If Van Deer's numbers are right, no. No way for *Columbia* to revisit *Excalibur* in time. Time looks to be very short, Steve. The hulk's weaving around now. So it looks like a revisit mission is out."

"What about a contingency plan?"

"Prayer. Fasting."

"Come on."

"There's nothing. They've kicked around some revisit schemes, trying to put a booster on *Excalibur* from *Columbia*, sending something up under ground control. Maybe they will.

But, really, I don't think anybody thinks we can get back to the derelict if it's this close to reentry. You remember *Skylab*. We just couldn't tell where we were, even though we had enough control at the end to bring that one back where it didn't hit anything but the middle of Australia. But we can't get control of *Excalibur*. Whatever happened . . . and nobody knows what happened up there, what killed our men . . . " He paused, thinking, I supposed, of the four men he knew, liked, and had lost to an impossible accident. Then, "Whatever happened destroyed our ability to control her. So in she'll come. She's *designed* to survive reentry. Okay, given some damage because of a bad angle of attack, she'll probably reenter more or less intact, so that at some point something the size of a DC–9 will crash somewhere. A lot of DC–9-sized objects have crashed without greatly changing anything, Steve."

"What'll she bring back, though? What was the payload?"

Silence. I heard him worrying that one. Finally he said, "It was military. Classified. We never knew."

"Bullshit."

"Look, I *know* we've called every military load since the fourth *Columbia* flight top secret. Maybe that cost us some credibility with the press. But this one was the real article, Steve. Even the astronauts weren't told about it until they were airborne. *Really* classified."

"I don't believe you, Les. Somebody in NASA has to do a wiring diagram, something. Of course you guys know the payload."

"Believe me or don't, it's the troof."

"Jesus. Okay . . . then what are the odds of its coming down on a large city?"

He told me those odds and those of being hit by a piece of *Excalibur*, ran back over the footprint, the orbital parameters, the sizes and weights of things that might reach the surface, the predictability of reentry, and on and on. When we were through I said, "First time I've had a NASA fact sheet read to me over the phone. Usually they just hand them out, like it's a free country."

Surprisingly, he laughed. "I guess we could mail you one right after your story breaks tomorrow."

"Les, for somebody surprised by a late-afternoon call, you've got a hell of a lot."

"We're on the ball."

"Bullshit."

"Let me go off the record here, Steve, okay?"

"Sure."

"We've been waiting for some sharp science writer to call. We help pay the Astrogeophysical Union's way. We see the abstracts. We knew what Van Deer was going to say. We even knew how to use the technique old Professor Andreev gave her at the ICSU meeting in Geneva last spring. We know we have a problem, and we wanted to let it sit as long as it could. There's no point in our making some big fucking announcement that the sky is falling, even if it is. We don't know when, or where, or even for sure. We think maybe we can even keep it from falling.

"The other thing is, we have a hundred-million-dollar unit designed to be operated by the Shuttle crew that can push *Excalibur* into a higher orbit where it'll fly for years and put people aboard to find out what the hell happened up there. Or, that failing, point it into the ocean on reentry. If we even recognize the *possibility* that the mission is futile, we get no bucks from the Congress to finish building the unit." His voice rested. I heard him listening.

"Can I ask a snide question?"

"What other kind is there?" A touch of frost, though.

"How come an agency like NASA, that measures every contingency down to a gnat's testicle, with the *Skylab* experience behind it, would overlook the rather glaring possibility that a hundred-ton spacecraft wouldn't burn up on reentry?"

"In a word, Steve, we fucked up."

"Come on. If a guy in the Pentagon told me that I'd just smile and nod. This one's really out of character for you guys. It's too big, too . . . gross."

"Be that as it may, fucked up is what we did. Nothing subtle. Nothing Satanic. Just a fuck-up." His voice had no reflection in it, no listening now. It made me believe him.

"What do I get when I do the real story—the one about fucking up in the first place?"

"A Pulitzer and two busted knees."

I laughed back. "Thanks, Les. You make it real attractive."

"Always glad to help."

We parted friends, which I hadn't expected.

After the talk with Dunham, I went down the hall to our library and asked Edna (the full-bodied) for her *Excalibur* file, and watched her hunt it out—always fun to watch Edna's moves. Then I went back to my station and spread things out as best I could in the clutter and began pecking out the story. I spent the early evening blessing old Les for making a tough piece so easy, and blessed him again when Mariela (the gaunt) had begun typing the story into the computer.

I lingered in the city room chatting with colleagues, screwing around, waiting to hear something from Horatio (the surly), my editor. But, really, waiting for an opportunity to talk to him about the larger stories, the sun, the NASA fuck-up. My unconscious turned these over, worried them, searching each visible side, asking why. And even back then, Danilov kept drifting in on the horizons of my questions, annoying and irrelevant as a horsefly, pushed here and there across my consciousness by mild grief.

Horatio called me over after a while and we talked about the story. He thought it might be important, which I thought was pretty intelligent of him, for him. In fact, we were only surface adversaries. I admired the older man, liked the way life had marked up his rutted face, veined the big nose, inoculated the dark eyes with knowledge of the world. He had done something clandestine during the Korean War, had parachuted into desperate times, the whole bit. He brought a hell of a lot more to his job than I did to mine. Now he wondered whether I had a next step in mind. I told him I was glad he'd asked that question and offered my package. "I need to look at two things. One's the solar part of the story. I'd like to do a piece on how and why they monitor the sun, what it means to everybody."

"Does it mean something to everybody?" He had sensed the approach of a request for travel, and now his big brown eyes clouded in their leathery pouches as he withdrew his interest systematically, inexorably, as though he drew in an anchor chain. His voice clattered and banged. "Who the hell cares?"

"People like sun things. Just as they like earthquakes and hurricanes. It'll do well. I promise."

"Oh well, if you *promise.*"

"Come on."

"What else?"

"Okay, the second part is why NASA made such a miscalculation in the first place. That's a hell of a story, Horatio."

"I like it better than the sun thing. Do it first." He wore the look of a man turning over an ace.

"They're interconnected. I need the sun thing to do the NASA story, and vice versa. It's a puzzle, man. One puzzle."

"I get the impression you can't do these from your chair in Miami?"

"You are perceptive, as ever. The solar part needs a few days at Alamo Peak. New Mexico. Where they monitor the sun. That's where the scientific paper came from that opened the shuttle story today. The other part means a trip to Washington, maybe Huntsville too. Mere bagatelles."

"Two trips."

"Maybe three."

"I'll talk to them about your bagatelles. Shall we have the pleasure of your company at work tomorrow?"

"Sure."

"I'll tell you what they say."

"Good."

"Later." He brushed me away with his hands and shook his head in avuncular fashion. I carried a feeling of his oldness away with me, a sense of something waiting for me that would make life less good. Poor Horatio.

On the way out I checked the wires, where, among all the triumph, collapse, and middling bullshit, we had news of an active sunspot region on the sun, with flares as big as the Ritz, aurorae over Cheyenne, and widespread radio and radar outages up north. A solar reminder. I thought about the energetic outburst from the sun reaching down to trouble *Excalibur*'s fragile orbit, cheating NASA out of x hours of orbital time to do their thing. I thought of the great tiled bird weaving along its shaky line two hundred miles up, carrying its dead astronauts, the micron or two of metal skin trembling infinitesimally beneath the solar touch. And of Danilov, dead somehow in space. It seemed to me then a random mixing of unconnected events; but there was no separating them, even that early in the game.

4

The night had swept my part of Miami with a burst of rain, which had moved off toward Hialeah and points north, where lightning flickered like distant artillery. Overhead the sky rose pale with stars. Everything glistened under the crime lights downtown, the mercury vapor lamps along the causeways. The air trembled with moist clarity, came cool to the touch, the only natural coolness you get in a Miami summer. It is a pretty city to cross by freeways, which, on the absolute flatness of southern Florida, are the only terrain. One seems to fly over Miami at helicopter altitudes, and the town lies bright and wonderful with light, the ocean glimmering beyond.

I'd missed lunch and by nine-thirty was hungry as hell, and so I got off at the Rickenbacker Causeway and drove down Bayshore for some seafood by the marina. The restaurant was one of those places where no one ever seems to know you, a place for boaters, with portholes instead of windows and spears and nets and saltwater aquaria scattered around the long room. I ate mightily of stuffed shrimp and salad, washed down with a half-carafe of the house chablis, and even went a piece of Key lime pie, food to push out the small, round tummy I'd developed by way of showing I had appetites. Through the meal I faced a sea-horse tank, watching the mournful creatures drift through their tiny world, anchoring here and there in the hope that the slight currents of the tank would float some food within range. We'd had sea-horses to watch the afternoon Danilov and I and the others went out at Cocoa, and the Russian had said, laughing, "They move like cosmonauts in space." His ghost still pursued me. I wondered why.

With the stomach taken care of, I examined my evening and the restlessness that had settled on me and decided to head for the Zodiak, where I could get a beer or two and be surrounded by beautiful women who took off their clothes. I headed out LeJeune, rain slicked and glaring with brake lights, and parked in back of the white stuccoed building that housed these delights. I found a seat at the bar where the three stages were in view and watched the place fill up with men arranged at tables facing each stage, watching, some of them slathering just a trifle, as three dancers did their different things. A black girl I didn't recognize who'd got everything off except a little bit of cloth across her biscuit did an energetic Caribbean number for one crowd, while Laurie, a tall, clumsy blond who had once helped me spend fifty bucks, did a modified teenybopper step for another. The third dancer was a beautiful friend named Marcia, who looked like Vanessa Redgrave but cared nothing for politics or much of anything else. Just very pretty, with clothing and without. I waved to her and she gave me the faintest hint of a smile, and danced her very slow and gentle dance. The pale blue dress she preferred to sequins draped a chair in the shadows behind her. Like all women who dance, she was larger than life while she was on the stage.

Joints like the Zodiak can be grim or fun, and the Zodiak was mostly fun, really a kind of men's bar with great decor. The dancers tricked a little on the side but earned enough dancing that they didn't have to; it wasn't one of those New York City lash-ups where you look around and find a black guy with a pink Continental running the girls twenty-four hours a day. The place was kid owned and kid operated, which is not to say kids can't be nasty too, but that good humor seemed to have prevailed. Although the girls weren't working their way through college, everybody was searching for something better, and the turnover was unbelievable. You didn't make any long-term attachments. Marcia had been there a couple of months and had a kind of constituency. But we all knew she'd disappear by winter. Penny, the skinny little bar girl with long blond pigtails and a face as hard as an adolescent refugee's, was an exceptional case—she'd been around for about six months. I always thought she'd wanted to dance and been found too lean, for the music kept her moving behind the bar. She smiled for me when she brought my beer and I asked her how she was doing. "Okay, Steve. I'm always okay. How about you?" And, without waiting to hear, she danced away to work.

They kept the place pretty dim. You could just see to read at the bar, where red and white light streamed out of star-shaped ceiling cutouts. The mirrors behind the dancers reflected some light from their spots (or strobes, if they were still funny about showing themselves without the camouflage of a flashing light). Still, the place stayed pretty dark. It took most of that first beer for my eyes to adjust and a few minutes more to notice that, if I looked just short of Marcia's stage, I peered into the fixed gaze of the big cop-eyed man named Cerf. It was like looking into the source of everything cold and cruel. I turned away quickly, excited and a little frightened, as from an unexpected brush with something large, slick, and alive in the sea.

I went back to watching Marcia, who finished her dance and put on the blue dress and panties. She came over barefooted. "Hey, Steve," she said in her soft, empty voice.

"Hey, beautiful lady." I realized I was making an effort at manliness, having just been scared by a big shadow.

She sat down on the adjacent stool, and Penny brought her a thin rum and tonic, the after-sundown equivalent of Gatorade. Up close I could see strain around Marcia's eyes, a paleness about the broad, sweet mouth. "You okay?" I asked.

"Oh, sure," she replied without conviction.

"You look a little bushed tonight."

"Thanks a heap, Steve."

"Beautiful, but bushed."

"Better." She smiled a little smile, but her mind focused somewhere, or on someone, else.

"You're acting like a lady with a problem."

"That figures."

"Want to talk?"

"I don't want to bring you in, Steve."

"Trouble?"

She nodded, watching the crowd, the hydra, around the stage

she'd go to next. I followed her look and saw the boyfriend, a big guy with forearms like thighs and a mean, stupid face framed in dark shoulder-length hair. Killer hippie. "He wants to carry you up the Empire State Building, right?"

It brought a gush of tickled laughter. "Right."

King Kong saw her laugh and frowned at us. I kept from staring too long into his eyes, figuring much directness would drive him toward violence, like a Doberman. "What happens after tonight?"

"He's sailing someplace tomorrow."

"Want to drop out?"

She shook her head. "I can do one night of trouble, Steve. But thanks. Thanks a bunch, really." She touched my arm with a long, lovely hand and slid off into the dimness, heading for the women's room. Kong looked after her and, apparently satisfied she was going to stay around, resumed flashing me his look of hatred. But when her music started and Marcia stepped into the spotlight, he stopped looking pissed, started staring at her, his mind losing me as swiftly as a reptile's.

Turning away from Kong, I found myself peering into a disconcerting closeup of police-eyes, who had settled himself just to port. "How are you this evening, Mr. Borg?" he asked in his slightly accented baritone, and slid onto the stool Marcia had warmed up.

"Just fine. Your name is Cerf?"

"I'm surprised you know that. But, yes, we were both at the press conference this afternoon."

"I remember."

Penny wriggled over and we ordered a couple of beers. Cerf moved his cold eyes from dancer to dancer, letting them linger on Marcia. "An extraordinary place."

"They're very pretty."

"And so plentiful. Are they available?"

"Some are hookers; some aren't. You just have to ask." Then, "This your first time here?"

"Yes. I am not often in Miami these days."

"Just down for the press conference?"

"Yes."

And then, because his reappearance in my life reminded me of my puzzle, I decided to press him a little. "You know, I had the impression you and Van Deer were connected at the briefing. I guess I thought you were an agency plant, but Randy Jones put you with . . ."

"International Earth-Space Enterprises," he interrupted.

"Yeah."

"No connection, Mr. Borg. Call me a gadfly. But when I read the abstract of Dr. Van Deer's paper, I knew we had an opportunity we would not have again. Now NASA must respond with some form of action—or, more likely, inaction."

"International Earth-Space Enterprises sounds like the cover for the antispace league."

"We believe there are problems space money could solve here on Earth."

He made my bullshit-detectors hum. Nothing in his cold eyes would spend a dime to spare the snail darter—or New York City either. His speech came off a record somewhere in his large frame and had the verisimilitude of words in a Steve Canyon balloon. I decided I had nothing to lose by telling him so. "I don't believe that."

Cerf laughed, a harsh, banging laugh, but his hard eyes grew harder. "Fair enough. Then let's let the matter rest where it was this afternoon."

"Leaving me to wonder how you fit in?"

"I have my own reasons for wanting the reentry story to go out."

"We can forget the gadfly bit?"

"Yes."

"Can we go further?"

"You have written your story?"

"Yep."

"Where do you go from here?"

For a moment I hesitated, wondering how open to be with this guy. Then I thought, what the hell, and said, "A piece on the sun itself. Another on the miscalculation."

"Which hypothesis do you choose?"

"I don't understand."

"You have to choose between hypotheses—the fuck-up or the conspiracy."

"I sort of incline toward the fuck-up hypothesis." In fact, I didn't believe in large conspiracies, doubting the ability of groups—committees, Klans, governments, corporations—to act so coherently.

"Perhaps I can help you."

"Why would you?"

"I like to see justice done." He gave an ugly chuckle. "In fact, that is one of the large truths about me. I am a person who likes to see justice done." For a time he radiated such cruelty I had to look away. His next words called me back. "Mr. Borg, I have to say I know ever so many interesting things about you. I know where and when you were born and about your parents and cousins and work. I know your undistinguished service history. I know you covered two years of the Vietnam war for the radical press. I understand why you would prefer to cover science. I know you corresponded with the late Soviet cosmonaut, Vladimir Danilov . . ."

"You're government."

"Yes."

"I don't trust government help."

"We need one another to solve this puzzle."

"Puzzle. That's how I've thought of it too."

"Because it *is* a puzzle, absolutely. I know some of it. Others know the rest. You may be the first to get it whole."

"You want a ferret."

"You want protection."

"Bullshit."

"Yes and no. And I want something back from you in this. I want to give you something, a few clues, since you are beginning a long time after some very good players, and you will need this help."

"And the strings?"

"You give me back what you discover." He grinned carnivorously. "Some of which I will already know."

"But . . . you reserve the right to follow me down the labyrinth?"

He laughed. "How skeptical you are, Mr. Borg. If I wanted to do that I could get farther in a day than you will in a year. But, you see, while I am only interested in seeing justice done, I have a point of view. Whereas you are a journalist. Objective. Idealistic. Unyielding." His laughter overtook his words.

"If you could, you would," I said, pissed that he'd laugh at me.

"You're right, Mr. Borg," he replied, suddenly serious and frightening again. "If I could, I would. Of course."

"In my heart, Cerf, I see it as an elaborate way to leak a story."

"Very perceptive of you."

"So, my man, give me your clue."

He leaned toward me then, as though to make our talk, already lost in the din, more confidential. "I have some terms for you. *Godfoot.* Do you know the term?" I shook my head. "Another: *Kiev Centre.*"

"Nothing," I said.

"And the third: *Bride Head.*"

"What every young girl should know?"

"Ask one of your better NASA contacts about these terms. He may or may not know them, but if he tells you positively there are no such things, he is lying."

"And you want to hear what I hear?" Sneeringly asked.

"Very much. Very much. For which, Mr. Borg, I promise you my protection."

"Protection. You keep coming back to that. I need less than you think."

"You need more than you know."

"Come on."

"Your work on this puzzle, this journey of yours into the labyrinth, will involve you with some very rough people."

"Like you?"

His eyes flashed racks and iron maidens. "Like me. I will try to stay out of sight but available. Now, good night." He left his seat like a bear getting off a circus stool and padded out into the evening.

I stayed where I was until after midnight, drinking beer and musing about the peculiar dream of a day I'd had, my mind thick with ramifications, the early exhilaration drained away by Cerf and all the complications he seemed to represent. I suddenly wanted out of everything, wanted to be able to come to my bar and watch the ladies dance and have my beer and not be beset by fucking G-men. First thing in the morning I'd tell Horatio there wasn't much story in this after all and go back to writing about weather and pollution in southern Florida.

Finally, after I asked her if I could untie her braids, Penny shooed me out to the bug, which took me home to my high rise on the water, a marbled glass and steel tower where I paid more than I should have for an alcoved kitchen and bath, the bed a pull-out affair nested in a big sofa, a counter to eat on, a corner to work in, some art along the white walls from sales down in the Grove. Barely home, like a lot of places men live in without sending out roots. But the light on the water at night, the bright days from the tiny balcony, the wind off the sea were fine, and I supposed I'd live there until the next hurricane blew it all away.

My dreams, when they arrived, were all busywork and anxiety, jobs I couldn't handle, places I couldn't find, a final exam in a math class I'd forgotten to attend all year; Randy Jones and John Chester, Les Dunham and Horatio, Cerf—my day's little cast of characters walked on and off my feverish set, like pilgrims threading through a mosque, with a worried Marcia dancing her distress, and everywhere, like the ghost of Hamlet's father, pervasive as smoke, the weightless presence of my friend Vlad Danilov.

5

The three terms had a life of their own. They lay like golden apples, fairy-tale apples, on the very rim of my mind. I sensed that they meant high excitement, play for large stakes, a way for young Boots to scale the glass hill—everything Steve Borg wanted then, back in that impossibly remote time when he still had a touch of youth and danger existed as an abstract quantity somewhere outside his realities. I let the golden apples lie. Sometimes I'd say, inadvertently, *"Godfoot,"* or *"Kiev Centre,"* or *"Bride Head,"* and then, unable to take it further, let them go, back to being golden apples. It was like being futilely in love, unable to see, hear, touch them enough and also unable to get near them. So I made my life go on, living with the exotic golden apples in my mind and some poor dreams to drive me. I lay low, storing my excitement over the sun and shuttle stories, I forgot management and my travel bagatelles, and so, apparently, did Horatio. I forgot about Sonya Van Deer's braid. Well, nearly. The weeks slid by, as they will whether you pursue a story or not.

I kept active. I covered a weather satellite launch at Kennedy and took Marcia along, with interesting results. I went on a two-day oceanographic promotion into the Gulf Stream, alone, and wrote it up. I did a piece on Key West sewage circling back to the beach and took Marcia with me when I researched the story. I did a series on the unusualness of winters, past and future. A short piece on Soviet killer satellites. Something on supernovae and the extinction of dinosaurs. Freon and the ozone shield. Dirigibles coming back. And on.

And I got to where I only dreamed of Cerf three nights in ten. He'd made an impression, and in his visitations he came on threatening, like the ghost of stories past, as if to say: Off your ass, Borg, and back to the work you're supposed to be doing. Rub them golden apples, man. I always woke up in a sweat, the details of the dream lost in anxiety back in sleep somewhere.

And there was the sun.

Every day brought news of more flares from forecasters at Boulder and Alamo Peak. The Wirephotos showed the big, blotchy disk in the red line of hydrogen, veinous, illuminated from the perpetual explosion within, the dark spots larger than Earth, the raw, bright free forms of enflamed plage larger than Jupiter. To me, focused subconsciously on the reentry problem, our star seemed to nibble away at *Excalibur*'s orbit, when really this was just the twenty-first cycle of solar activity heating up. But the sun's violent behavior sized the fuze for the dead shuttle's orbit, defined our terms, gave us a countdown.

Godfoot. Kiev Centre. Bride Head.

I wrote them down in doodles, margined my prose with them, but took them nowhere. I kept the *Excalibur* file on my desk and pawed around in it occasionally, and got out the Apollo–Soyuz press kit that had Danilov's brief bio and took it home—purely a sentimental gesture, I thought, but also a reflexive part of working the puzzle.

NASA kept active too. It released to the world its view that it might have got hold of *Excalibur* after all, might boost it farther out, or bring it into the ocean . . . something. The story was theirs, and they played it every fifth day or so: the attempted smoothings of a decaying orbit, the optimism, the pessimism, back and forth, drawing it out to get that appropriated money into the pipeline for an impossible rescue mission.

Abruptly the agency waxed optimistic about bringing the big hulk safely back into the sea, hurting no one. But, to us casual observers, the waxing looked self-destructive, like the growth of a red giant. A week later one of the famous NASA program managers said it wasn't possible to do shit about *Excalibur*. A day after that the agency head said the hell it wasn't. In ten days NASA announced it could still get up there and boost the hulk to a higher orbit, save a bunch of money by using it over and over again, adding it would also permit us to bury our American dead, Jesus. We winked and nudged one another down at the *Herald*. A fortnight later, following a flurry of fiscal infighting among Congress people and additional dire forecasts of heavy solar activity by Sonya Van Deer's organization, NASA announced it was going to forget the whole thing and reminded everyone there was little chance of being hurt when *Excalibur* came in, most of the Earth being covered with ocean and all. At that point the reentry stabilized as nothing much more than a major media event, and things got quiet on the shuttle front as the wires and papers and networks calculated how to cover the reentry and from where.

This was in late July, when the North American Air Defense Command (NORAD) began issuing its periodic forecasts of when and where *Excalibur* would reenter. They initially put the reentry into mid-September, then back into early August; then NASA repredicted the whole thing and said it would be toward the end of August. Every few days the forecast would shift the reentry point by half a hemisphere and tell us *Excalibur* was now losing two thousand, then three thousand, feet per day; the wires kept the forecasts coming: Everything is news.

The first NORAD forecasts, I suppose, were the kind of signal I'd needed to remind me that from the first day, like a man in love, I'd thought deeply, unconsciously, of little else. I came back to life.

I asked Horatio about the travel. He radiated surprise and said he'd look into it.

And I called Les Dunham again. "I'd hoped somebody'd call about that fucking story," he said, meaning the story that they were going to leave *Excalibur* alone. Then he waited without wondering to find out why I'd called.

"I was calling about the larger story, Les. The fuck-up story, as it's known in the trade."

"Ah, *that* story." The fun drained from his voice as he went on guard.

"The same. It occurred to me while all this try, untry, and surrender have been going down . . ."

"If I had your way with words, Steve . . ."

"You'd've been a writer. But it came to me that at some point we have to go ahead and choose between a fuck-up and a, uh, conspiracy." It startled me to be using Cerf's vocabulary.

"Ugly term."

"An alternative term to fuck-up is all. I mean, given a hundred tons circling in orbit, there ought to be some plan—some ploy maybe—to squeeze out more money, to get people to evacuate southern California. I don't know. Something."

"Yeah, Steve, we'd like to harness all that momentum all right. Did you call to talk, or what?"

"I want to try three terms on you, Les. Give me some free association. Off the record, okay?"

"Shoot." He sounded as relaxed as William Tell's son.

"*Godfoot.*"

"Sorry, Steve." I heard relief in his voice.

"Never heard of it?"

"Nope."

"*Kiev Centre.*"

"Russian shopping mall?"

"Nothing?"

"Nothing."

"*Bride Head.*"

I got a tremor, a magnitude two or three tremor out of him on that. He said, "Nor that," but I heard the slight shift of tone, a slurring, whatever the sound is we make when we lie.

"Les, I believe you on numbers one and two. I think you're shitting me on number three."

"Your right to believe that is protected by the Constitution, Steve." Then, pausing slightly, he asked, "Can I ask where you got your terms?"

"Why?"

"No reason."

"Oh, of course not. An angel brought them in a vision, man."

"I can dig that."

"Look, Les, I'm not dumb. I'm going to figure this out. It's just a matter of time."

He laughed. "You're so right, Steve."

I hung up.

And then, as I sat there steaming about Dunham and government in general, Randy Jones called. I picked it up, annoyed at having my concentration interrupted but unwilling to be snotty to my old, pitiful pal. "Hey, Randy," I exclaimed like a boy.

"Hi, Steve."

"Where are you?"

"Back in town for the chem society."

"That's a big society."

"We all make mistakes."

"Right." We laughed. Then, "What can I do for you, lady?"

"I wondered when you're coming to Santa Fe."

"I'm working on it. Management has to approve my travel. Takes years."

"You doing a sun story?"

"Yep, and one on why they got so fucked up to begin with. Maybe. I don't know."

"You sound like you're losing your finely honed edge, Steve."

"Yeah, I know. The shuttle thing is full of weird happenings. Unnatural acts."

"But interesting." She wanted more.

"Oh, really. Interesting, sure." I decided not to give it.

"Is this something you should leave alone?" Her reflex: to warn me off.

"You mean, Protecting Our Side?"

"I guess."

"I can't tell," adding, "Who gives a shit about Sides?"

"So when're you coming down?"

"To Santa Fe? Maybe in August. Maybe sooner."

"I hope I'm around. Don't come without letting me know. But plan to stay at my place. Lots of room. No emotional claims. Southwestern cuisine, whatever that is."

"Sounds great." It sounded lonesome, too. "I accept. What about you, you going to be around Miami awhile?"

"Fly home on a red-eye tonight."

"Reconsider and I'll buy your dinner."

"No, I really can't, Steve."

And I, relieved to have the burden going home quickly, "Maybe next time."

And she, understanding each familiar move, "I'll take a rain check."

"Fine. Glad you called, kid."

"Me too. Take care."

"Bye."

"Bye." Her voice went small at the end of our talk. Again, I sensed regret, but at that point I thought it had to do with missing a rare evening with a wonderful guy.

But I wasn't concentrating on Randy. While we talked I'd been spreading my notes, the pocket-sized scraps and yellow legal-sized sheets on which doodles and scribbled words and phrases circled one another, handwriting I had to put in better form before it turned into a bunch of wavy little lines I couldn't read. I wrote:

1. *These all have to connect with the shuttle reentry.*
2. *There seem to be two sides.*
3. *How many things on each side link up, if any?*

Then I made a *Them* and *Us* column, noting: *Are them us? Are us U.S.?* Under *Us* I put me, Sonya Van Deer, Les Dunham. What the hell, Randy Jones, since she called. Cerf under *Them*. And on, trying to get everything even tangentially connected into a matrix of sense, and yes, thinking, Goddamn it, Dunham, I'm *not* dumb. I *will* figure this out . . .

The golden apples I also tried to allocate. But it didn't work. I wrote *Kiev Centre* and *Godfoot* in the margin, adding Andreev and John Chester and Danilov. And *Bride Head*—I had trouble with that one. It sounded like a word but wasn't, as the old second edition confirmed. Still, it was familiar. And then I thought: *Brideshead*, with an *s*. Cerf probably thought the term was like maidenhead because English was his second (or tenth) language. He spoke it but didn't read its novels. *Brideshead Revisited*. Sum bitch, I thought; revisit mission had been Dunham's term. Sum *bitch*! I put *Brideshead* under *Us* with an exclamation point and called Les Dunham.

When he came on, I said, "I broke your code, boy."

"Sorry to hear that, Steve. Mind elaborating?" A very neutral voice.

"*Bride Head*. It's *Brideshead*, with an *s*. A revisit mission."

"No comment."

"Want to hear my lead?"

"Sure."

" 'Despite yesterday's announcement that no further effort would be made to control space shuttle *Excalibur*'s decaying orbit, the National Aeronautics and Space Administration continues to ready a clandestine mission to revisit the derelict space station . . .' "

"You never could write a lead."

"It goes on, man. 'Dubbed "Brideshead" by agency scientists, after the Evelyn Waugh novel, *Brideshead Revisited*, the project . . .' "

"Look, I told you we had some revisit missions penciled in. We scrubbed them. *Brideshead* was one of them. It's over."

"If you'd said that the first time we talked I'd believe you, old buddy. But you can't stonewall me on this until I get you by the balls and then suddenly be open and informative and say it used to be important but isn't any longer. Come on."

"But it's crap, Steve. You can't print that kind of crap."

"I can. I will. I'll shove a big fucking light right up your *Brideshead*, boy. You want to revisit, you best keep me from running this thing. Period."

Silence. Then, behind his cupped hand I felt the sigh I couldn't hear. "Steve," he said, "I need a little time on this one."

"Why?"

"This thing we're talking about isn't . . . widely known around the agency, okay? A few good men and women. I have to talk to them. Then I promise to bring you in. Exclusively."

"How about if I give you a couple of hours?"

"How about forty-eight?"

"That only means you'll have done your thing in thirty-six, my friend. What I'll do is write the piece with what I have. If you don't get back to me in a couple of hours it goes in tomorrow's

Herald, and you can spend Thursday explaining about misappropriation of appropriated funds. If you do get back to me I may not run it for another day or two, depending on what you have."

More silence. Then, through clenched teeth, "I'll call back in a couple hours."

"Thanks, Les."

"Fuck you, Steve."

It left me higher than hell, to have got that far, and warm brained, ready for more. Sure enough, the gray electrochemical mess, in its warmed-up state, brought forth the ghost of Danilov once more, who whispered: *Godfoot.*

6

I got home by midafternoon, poured a hundred cc's of Scotch, and made a peanut-butter and mayo sandwich, what my mother always called a Dead Sandwich, and began my Danilovian review. First I took out the NASA press kit on Apollo–Soyuz and read of the third crew:

Flight Engineer—Danilov Vladimir Sergeevich
Captain Vladimir Sergeevich Danilov, USSR space pilot, Hero of the Soviet Union, was born in 1942 in the town of Cistopol, Tambov Oblast region, Central Tatar A.S.S.R.

In 1959 Vladimir graduated from a secondary school with a Gold Medal and entered S. Ordzhonikidze Moscow Aviation Institute. After the graduation from the Institute, Vladimir began working in solar astronomy at the Hydrometeorological Institute facility near Moscow, where he revealed comprehensive knowledge and aptitude for scientific research and published in scientific journals. In 1965 Vladimir entered an aviation school. He graduated from it with an honors diploma and became a professional military pilot.

In January 1968 he joined the Communist Party of the Soviet Union.

In January 1969 he was named to cosmonaut corps.

Danilov is an honorary citizen of towns: Cistopol, Karaganda, Kaluga, Ostrogozhsk, Arkalyk, Houston.

V. Danilov continues his solar astronomy researches. He is also an expert aerobatic sport pilot and a good car driver.

Rewards: Order of Lenin, one "Gold Star" medal of Hero of the Soviet Union, Gold Medal of Tsiolkovskiy (from the USSR Academy of Sciences), Gold Medal of the Ukrania SSR Academy of Sciences, and others.

That was the Soviet version of Vlad, written in the inimitable style of some Soviet flack writing in English, a style that sometimes makes us underrate them. Mine had him warmer, less in their organization, perhaps . . . although, who knew? Not me. It was just that, as my thoughts pivoted on the matter of the shuttle reentry, he glided into them more and more, haunting me.

Godfoot, I thought, and went for his letters, shuffled into my nest of bills and scraps of stories and new names and phones, written late at night usually, hard to read. If I'd been less Roman and more Greek, I would have sensed the omens working here. But as it was, when I spread out the four little envelopes from Danilov before me, they seemed unportentous. Each was addressed to me care of my mother in the venerably ugly town of Cairo, Illinois, where my rivers conflowed. I suppose (but don't really remember) I gave him the address.

The first letter came in the spring of 1975, from New York, where Danilov and some of his fellow cosmonauts had spent a few days on some space promotion linked to the Apollo–Soyuz shot.

Dear Friend Steven,

I am in New York for a few days and am writing to you. This could come to you as a surprise, since we scarcely know each other yet. Still, I was feeling after our day in Florida that we can be friends. That is why I am writing, to let you know that you have a friend who is a U.S.S.R. Cosmonaut. This one is not going up in the Apollo– Soyuz after all. We are here to talk on the television about the mission. We will be here three or four days. Then we go to Florida for the mission. Some of us will watch. I hope I can see you there.

Somebody else covered Apollo–Soyuz, I remembered. Something kept me away, I forget what. Apathy, maybe. But I sent a note to Vlad through John Chester at NASA.

There is another reason for my writing, Steven. That is something we spoke of that afternoon. Remember we spoke of personal liberty in my country and in yours. To be frank, I do not remember if we had acrimony between us on this subject. I am very much wishing for you to understand that at heart I am not very totalitarian at all. And you also must not have been what you at first seemed. I hope we can be "Pen Pals" at least.

I laid aside the letter and thought back to that afternoon to the half-remembered dark spot in all the good humor. But I still couldn't remember what he'd said. I picked up another letter and let the mnemonic circuits go to work.

Dear Friend Steven,

Thank you for trying to respond to my first letter written last spring from New York. I think that on the whole it is better you do not try to write me in the Soviet Union. The letters reach me but with a frown, if you are following my meaning. I write today from Helsinki. I am here because the meeting is on solar astronomy, which was my specialty before I became U.S.S.R. Cosmonaut. . . .

My unconscious intruded with the beginning of a memory: *Godfoot.* I worried it further and got something like, "Don't be talking to me about intrigue, Steven. Here we are all of us sitting, you and John Chester and Randy Jones and I. Between us we may be all representing quite a lot of intrigue. Quite a lot. Here . . . ask John Chester about *Godfoot* sometime when you want to be cynical.

I'd first heard the term that afternoon at Cocoa, from Danilov.

My memory coughed up something more. John Chester had made a gesture then, a nearly imperceptible hand sign for silence—the kind of signal you'd give a dog—and my stocky drunk Russian went quiet. *That* was a memory worth having.

. . . Speaking here today is Prof. Andreev, with whom I had breakfast, as well as with a woman I believe is his daughter, although they were at some pains to conceal it, why I am not knowing why. He taught me in solar physics in school, and I am admiring him for a

long time, we try to stay in touch although I am not of the field just now . . .

It took a moment to remember who Andreev was; then it came from the warm brain—the solar physicist whose method Sonya Van Deer had used to arrive at her prediction of a highly active solar cycle. The sun again. I shook my head with mild wonder. These notes from Danilov—and notes was all they were, scrawled on the small stationery of hotels in a boy's slanting, broad-blue script—were so innocent the first time and so laden now.

. . . I still worry about our last (our only so far) conversation. At first I believed you were simply being oblique about your involvements. Since then I am beginning to believe you are not being really involved at all . . .

The first time I'd read that I'd gone through quickly and interpreted *involvement* in the kid sense of either caring (involved) or uncaring (uninvolved). I hadn't asked myself: Involved in what?

. . . Therefore, I am feeling a need to have this set to rights, even after such a long time. I believed that day I was speaking to a captive, even though you are an American journalist and presumably as free as a man can be in some respects. Today I am believing more that you are as free as you appeared. I am happy to have such a free person for my friend. Someday I am wanting very much to sit with you again and tell you more about my life and my work, not in a political way, but friend to friend. Perhaps soon I am coming to the U.S.A. again and we can do this. Until then, I remain, your "Pen Pal."

I'd never reconciled the meager friendship strung between us with the larger friendship he evoked in his notes; it was as if we shared an army tour or a year in college, which I'd somehow forgotten. I guess I thought part of it was his wanting the occasional ear of an American reporter, something in the bank in case things went sour at home. Not that I could have done anything for him, but people on the outside don't always appreciate one's limitations. Reading his letter now, they were all hints, as though he urged me to reconstruct carefully our single face-to-face conversation, parse the dialogue, and find what he suggested—which I still could not see, beyond the reference to *Godfoot*.

The third letter came from Moscow.

Dear Friend Steven,

It has been nearly a year since I have written and I do so to wish you a very fine Christmas and best wishes for the New Year. Your card came. I especially liked the painting on it, it recalled the countryside centred on Kiev. There is a chance that I shall be in Florida later in the year, and I shall certainly give you a call if I can. Your friend . . .

There had been no card, and at the time I pondered briefly what he'd meant, being cryptic about the countryside centered on Kiev. Now, without knowing more than that he'd flagged it, I saw it said *Kiev Centre.*

He never arrived; but not quite a year ago this letter had, from Geneva.

Dear Friend Steven,

I am in Geneva for a week for another solar conference. Prof. Andreev is here—that is a name you should remember from my letter of more than a year ago—with his grown daughter, a very beautiful woman who it turns out is also a solar astronomer. I like this city very well, although it has its share of intrigue. I spend some time drinking and watching the Rhone run out of the lake. I need a river going somewhere in the background, as you told me of yourself.

Life is going well for me. I am once again beginning active Cosmonaut training and it looks as if exciting missions lie ahead of me finally, although I cannot say when or tell you what they are.

Often when I am in space I talk to you, Steven, knowing your ear is open and still free. Sometime in your sleep you may hear me say to you that the Earth is shining beautifully, or the sky is falling, or I am undone . . .

Hinting, hinting. But the sense of it went by me, like German, almost intelligible but nothing I could read.

. . . Of course, at such times I say mainly what I think you would like to hear . . .

Was he defining the purpose of the correspondence now?

. . . without going into any deeper meanings of the Cosmos, or whether we see ghosts in space, or the string of gravity that holds us up or pulls us down, the solar wind that drags us Earthward . . .

Again, the sun. A herald of *Excalibur* falling?

. . . To tell the truth I am growing more poetic by the year. I often wish we had not had that luncheon in Cocoa . . . no, I mean to say, I often wish we had shared our lunch alone. I still hope to see you someday, my friend.

That last, hurried, less-coherent paragraph was it, the end of Danilov. I looked at my notes:

I must not be what I seemed. Andreev. Daughter. Godfoot. Chester signal. Involved? Name I should remember: Andreev. Daughter again. Intrigue again? Ghosts, equal spooks? What he thinks I'd like to hear. Sky is falling.

I went back through the letters quickly, and added:

I am undone.

7

Back at the paper by seven-thirty I found notes to return a call to Les Dunham and to see Horatio if I could find the time. I called Dunham at his office and waited for him to tell me he was in. He did, grudgingly of course, and said, "I don't want to give you a full briefing over the phone, Steve."

"Phone's all we got."

"All you want is your pound of flesh, right?"

"Please, no ethnic references. I'm just your average WASP reporter."

"Sure, pal. Hold on a minute." He set the phone down at his end, and I heard doors sliding closed across the hollow silence of the receiver. Then he returned. "The people want you to consider holding your silence until *Brideshead* takes place, Steve. They'll involve you in it. They'll let you watch it happen. Everything. But they desperately want your silence until it happens."

"I'll consider it."

"Okay. You had it right, you know."

"Good." But the admission surprised me; I'd thought it a ball-park sort of accuracy at best.

"Maybe you didn't know. Maybe you pokered us into this, you son of a bitch."

"Please, just the news."

Dunham told me about *Brideshead*. A group of scientists at NASA's Marshall Space Center in Huntsville, Alabama, had detected the reentry problem: Given an active sun, *Excalibur* would return months earlier than expected. They'd sought funds through channels for a rescue mission—what they'd called a revisit mission—and got nowhere. Either *Columbia* would revisit or nothing would. Besides the problem came through the budget documents as too soft, and nobody wanted to sink a few million into saving a derelict that might or might not be reused.

"What about all the shit that could come back in during reentry?" I asked him.

"Nobody saw that as much of a problem. I mean, they weighed the risks and thought they were minimal. Which, I hasten to add, they are."

"Doesn't that sound kind of funny to you?"

"Steve, everything in government science sounds kind of funny to me. The Alabama lawyers on our subcommittee just didn't see it as a problem worth solving. Not like putting up a fucking dam or something."

"Okay, didn't mean to excite you."

"Shit." And he went on. Officially, the agency picked up the idea of an *Excalibur* rescue and ran with it, getting as far as the funds Dunham had described to me earlier—the remotely operated booster that a shuttle pilot could maneuver over to the derelict, hook it on, and blast the bulk either into a certain ocean landing or into a higher orbit that would last another decade or two. But no one had much hope for that one, since it coupled to *Columbia*, and the old ship's schedule kept slipping back in time at about the same rate as *Excalibur*'s reentry advanced. "We still had the money in the pipeline, though," Dunham said. "Then dear Doctor Van Deer fucked everything up with her solar forecast. If the sunspot numbers go that high, that early in the new cycle of activity, there's absolutely no chance of *Excalibur* staying up long enough for us to do anything about it. That was the official position, okay?"

"Okay."

But the Huntsville Group, as Dunham called them, had unofficially gone ahead with their rescue mission. "They took some funds here, some there, recruited some good heads from other centers, spliced the old Skylab team back together, and developed a plan they called *Brideshead*, I guess because one of the scientists had once read or heard of the Waugh novel.

"Anyway, *Brideshead* was planned as a limited Apollo mission, minus astronauts, minus life-support systems and all that other heavy stuff. A stripped leftover Apollo command module would be flown as a robot, maneuvered to inspect *Excalibur,* then to dock with the hulk, and use its engines to slow it down for a controlled reentry." Using names and cost-accounting numbers and key people from other, legal projects, he went on, the Huntsville Group had succeeded in getting the module, which had been camouflaged with some long folding antennae and various bumps and portals to pass for an X-ray astronomy vehicle, onto a Titan III booster and onto a pad at Kennedy. "We're within about a day of the shot, Steve. We want you to wait until we're through before you blow your whistle. In exchange, we'll fly you over to Huntsville in one of the Lears and let you go through the whole mission with us. Exclusively."

"You're on."

"Okay. That's good. But listen, I don't think twenty people in the agency know about this thing. You've got to keep it close until it's over. Really."

"I understand, Les. Thanks for cooperating."

"I guess I'm glad there's going to be a reporter in on this one. What the hell, it's a positive story. We used initiative, risked careers, misappropriated funds, but we did a can-do job to keep that ship from raining down on somebody's town."

"Agreed."

"The Lear'll pick you up at the general aviation terminal at Miami International at noon tomorrow. Okay?"

"Good. Fine." I laughed like a boy. "I'm delighted."

"I'll bet you are. Well, like the man said, It's been a business doing pleasure with you, Steve."

"Likewise. Bye." Then, "Oh, Les."

"Yeah?"

"You ever see John Chester?"

"Chester? All the time."

"Tell him I need to talk to him about *Godfoot.*"

"You're a greedy fucking doll, Steve." He hung up.

Feeling very much the neat guy, I marched over to Horatio's desk. "You rang?"

He looked me over unenthusiastically. "Nice of you to stop by."

I nodded obedient servantwise.

"Management says you can do the stories . . ."

"Good."

"But you got to bring back more from Alamo Peak than some sun thing. Promise two or three science pieces?"

"I've got a better deal now, man. NASA's flying me to Huntsville tomorrow. It's going to be a hell of a story."

"What story?"

"More of the *Excalibur* reentry."

"What, they're bringing in the whole science press corps?"

"Nope, just little me."

"Explain."

"I told Les Dunham I'd show some nude pix to his wife . . ."

"Come on."

". . . who has a heart condition . . ."

"You're not going if you don't tell me."

". . . and who's a Baptist besides."

"I'm serious."

"There'll be other papers, *viejo.*"

"That good?"

"Yessir."

"When do we get it?"

"When I get back."

"Which is . . .?"

"Today's Tuesday. I'll be back Friday, maybe sooner."

The day's work left me high indeed. Reporters were beginning to fan out, driven by the NORAD forecasts of when and where the sky would fall, desperately trying to get a purchase on a story that would happen out of human sight, possibly without human knowledge—*Excalibur* could come in when it was off the American radars, after all. And I, all by myself, was going to see NASA try to erase the threat with a daring, illegal, secret revisit mission. "Jesus *Christ!*" I whispered at my typewriter.

Even Chester's call failed to chill me, but just barely. I picked up the phone, listened to silence for a moment, then got John's pansy voice, nasty and complaining. "John Chester, here, Steve. I got your message."

"Good." My neck hairs rippled.

"You wanted to talk."

"About *Godfoot.*"

"So . . . talk about it."

"I'm doing a story on *Godfoot.*" Pause. Silence. "I got the details from Vlad Danilov, in a letter."

"He's dead."

"You don't sound very sorry."

"Let's say we had a quarrel." He made it sound gay. I thought of the thoroughly straight Russian and wondered why.

"Anyway, I'm doing a story."

"Good, Steve, go to it."

"I though you could fill in some of the details . . ."

"Like what?"

"Like," and I raced along, trying to think what the hell to ask, finally arriving at, "like, did *Godfoot* go into the original shuttle design?" In retrospect this seems prescient as hell, but in fact I just wanted to give him a *Godfoot* sentence with shuttle in it, since they seemed to be connected.

"I don't guess I can answer that one, Steve." A very cold voice, gone colder.

"Let's try another. Is *Godfoot* a NASA project?" Another gamble. I didn't know if it was a project or a kind of pipe fitting.

"Or that one. Look, Steve, I'm not being much help to you, buddy." The cold voice being friendly. "Let me get one of the people who really knows about *Godfoot* to talk to you. Can they call you tomorrow? It's pretty late here to get anybody."

"That's fine, John. I'll be in the office till about midday. Then I'm leaving town. I want to wrap it up before then." Bluff, bluff.

"I'm sure it'll be wrapped up by then." He said good-bye. I could feel his anger all the way from D.C., tickling the wire.

"Sum *bitch,*" I said, extremely pleased with old Steven Borg. Good work, proof of intelligence, evidence of great chutzpah, the working of a difficult puzzle. Jesus, it had been a fine day's work. It left me with the big shit-eating grin of a lover—the sight of myself reflected in a partition window made me smile with admiration. *There* went a man destined for food, drink, and the well-deserved affections of a pretty woman.

As it turned out, it was a drink, a meal, and a murder.

But who can read the future?

8

Like any red-blooded American boy, I wound up about ten-thirty nursing a beer at the Zodiak while a pale girl in black lace took it off under the strobes, filling the hall with boos. The strobes were a way of getting acclimated to your own nudity, and most of the dancers began with them, then graduated to baby spots and a kind of serious waving around of bottoms. A black girl who'd graduated swung hers like a mace on stage two, twirling feverishly in a naked dance that carried more than a little contempt for slathering honkey males. A large-breasted German woman of forty beat it out behind me; a lot of heat, no light, little humor. But what the hell, I'd had a day of days and wasn't really thinking about much except how great I was at my work and how poor these flacks and demispooks were at theirs. So that when Penny two-stepped over to my part of the bar and asked, "How's your mom, Steve-o?" I didn't notice the worry lines above her tough little eyes, but said something like, Wow, *que* sentimental, Penny.

"Say, speaking of moms," she added as an artificial afterthought, "I saw a good friend of yours tonight. . . ."

She got my attention. "What's up, Penny?"

"Marcia's out back, Steve," she replied, very low. "Needs some help I believe."

Marcia stood in a dark pocket behind the place, a beautiful statue in a field of cars, harsh shadows, and mercury lamps. She wore the light blue dress she seemed always to wear to work and looked okay at first. I said, "Hi," and she murmured something back at me. But when I touched her chin gently with my fingers she winced away. For an instant I saw her face in one of the harsh bands of light that fenced us. An ugly swelling darkened her left eye; the other gleamed with an eternity of crying. Her stance favored bruises you couldn't see.

"Home is the sailor," I said.

She nodded and released a muted cry.

"Okay, you get out of it tonight. Go to my place. Take my car." I wrapped her fingers around my keys.

"What about you?"

"I'll get a cab. Maybe I can ravish you. Bathe you. Something."

"Maybe."

"Go on, though."

"Thanks, Steve," she said. I waited while she found the bug, watched her out of sight down the tunnel of light along LeJeune, and went back to my beer.

I saw King Kong setting up shop at a table where the pale girl had finished dancing, and he gave me the empty look of hatred you get from these heroes. But when Marcia's music began and another girl filled in for her, his eyes looked at me with sudden understanding, like the eyes of an alligator registering last week's pain, and he raised himself and came over. For a threatening moment he just loomed, letting me sense his belief that he could kill me with a pair of well-placed blows; a strictly redundant show of force. "Where's Marcie?" he asked in one of those surprisingly high voices you hear from giant linemen.

"Don't know, man." I looked into his stupid, homicidal eyes, scanned the place for the bouncers, hoping their antennae were out for this kind of confrontation and that they'd break it up before he tore my suit.

"She avoiding me?"

"Don't know, bro."

"Come off it. You know where she went, man." I felt the ugly moment settle upon us and flinched away; but the giant hand got the back of my jacket and brought my head around where he could batter it.

"Hey, man, leggo . . ." The Borg Technique was to keep the

guy talking. A talking bully is an immobilized bully. But he'd gone quiet and wanted to break something, so he caught me, hard, with the heel of his hand on one cheek, snapping my head back. I kicked at his nuts a couple of times and he showed me his forehand. This fucker's going to kill me! my warm brain yelled into the spiral of light and pain.

"Enough!" someone commanded, grunting a little as he spoke. Half blind from the blows I could only see motion at first; then, as my vision cleared I picked out Kong himself down on all fours over a puddle of bile and blood, which poured from a broken nose. He looked like somebody's big sick dog down there. Jesus, I thought, I must've connected. But, no. My grizzly protector towered over him, his cold visage decorated to the south with a gold-toothed grin.

"Thanks," I whispered sincerely, feeling my face. "Thanks a bunch."

"You're welcome, Mr. Borg," he replied, moving onto the next stool.

"Can I buy you a drink?"

"A beer is fine, Mr. Borg, thank you."

The bouncers were dragging the wreck outside. I listened: The music, the dancing, the roar of conversation hadn't missed a beat. When Penny brought our beers I told her, "I'm real sorry for disrupting things."

"Don't be sarcastic, Steve-o."

"Were you actually going to let that monkey pound me into the floor?"

"Actually, I didn't think I'd be much help, Steve. But our boys was moving in."

"Not very damned fast."

"Come on, man. We ain't lost one yet. Even accident-prone ones like you." She giggled and twisted off to another corner of the bar.

"I take it, Mr. Borg, that you sent his woman somewhere," Cerf said. I nodded. "To your own apartment?"

"Yes."

"In your car?"

"Yep."

"It appears God is protecting you as well. That will turn out to have been a very wise move, Mr. Borg. At least as far as you are concerned." He moved his cold eyes over the crowd, then back to me. "But it has been some time since we talked."

"Yes, yes it has. How've you been."

"Very well, Mr. Borg. Very well indeed." He grinned gold for me. "And how is your puzzle coming along?"

"Oh . . . some progress here and there."

"Good." His eyes waited for a report and said he would not forgive my keeping anything back. "Did my clues help at all?"

"Yes, thanks."

"Well?"

"I've talked to a NASA guy about *Godfoot*. He's getting back to me tomorrow."

Cerf shuddered with contained anger. "And the others?"

"Nothing on *Kiev Centre*. I'm pushing another NASA contact on, uh, *Bride Head*." I pronounced it his way. "I should know more about that in another day or two."

His eyes flashed his knowledge of my lie. "And now you are about to take your first real steps into the labyrinth itself?"

Wondering how he knew, I nodded.

"Good," he said. "I think you will find now that things get a little rough, Mr. Borg. I have given you some protection, and you have given me nothing in return. So now you will have to look after yourself. Good luck."

Having saved another rancher from another bully and had his beer, my Lone Ranger set out, and his departure pretty much made my evening. My face throbbed where Marcia's boyfriend slugged me, and my warm brain had gone turbid with fatigue and a victim's despair. So I told Penny good-bye, dragged myself out into the brightly lighted night, and found a cab to take me back to my tower on the bay.

But in the elevator I remembered Cerf's telling me how wise it had been to send Marcia home in my car ahead of me, and the hairs on my neck prickled like a dog's. I ran down the long nightmare hall of doors to my own white metal one, discovered I had no keys and began to hammer, and wait, and curse, and knock again, thinking, Goddamnit Marcia, come *on,* feeling the need to take a leak, knocking again, rattling the doorknob . . .

The place was unlocked. The door pushed open beneath my startled hand. I entered gingerly, sensing that my steps took me into what Cerf had called the labyrinth itself, afraid of what I might find.

PART TWO

The great star trembles,
Ready to fall,
The Godfoot.
The people watch from their shadows,
Readying rockets for
Cosmonaut sappers
To keep the star from
Kiev Centre.
            Vladimir Sergeevich Danilov,
                U.S.S.R. Cosmonaut

1

Marcia had made herself at home, had a sandwich, left the mayonnaise out, had a Coke, smoked a joint, enjoying a night off, a night without trouble. She'd wrapped her beautiful self in my white terry-cloth robe and curled up not quite fetally on the pull-out bed and slept, expecting to be awakened when I came in, maybe ravished. Now she slept eternally in a room stinking with cordite and the meaty odors of violent death.

The killer had entered in darkness, blown away the sleeping figure. A hurried killing, an excited or frightened one perhaps, with slugs in the body, slugs in the wall.

The five that hit her left little red free forms in the terry cloth, stitched up the fine curve of her back into the delicate indentations at the base of her neck and into the skull. Three more slugs had smashed into the wall beyond the bed. Most of the gore spread on this far side; she watched it steadily with startled, dead green eyes. I touched her on the arm, which lay along the curve of her hip, a cold heavy arm. And then I knelt and put my head upon her covered thigh and tried to imagine her alive, tried to will her back to life with memories, and wanted to cry; but the loss of her had emptied me out, and the violence of it had left me only cold and frightened and lonely. My mind had begun to fill with dead friends, who die over and over in my haunted dreams; and yet there were no tears for Marcia.

I stayed with her for a time, until the coldness of her stung me through the terry cloth and forced me to acknowledge that nothing lived there anymore. Then I opened the balcony doors to let the salt air cleanse the room of death and, in a voice that barely worked, called the police to report my lady's murder. Afterward I stretched on the balcony chaise, watching the nighttime ocean and its knives of light.

They got there pretty fast, and I spent the rest of the early morning reconstructing Marcia's evening, and mine, for them, gave them Kong the Killer, told them I had no enemies this violent. Then they went on doing their thing around the apartment. Later one of them brought me my keys. By dawn they'd fingerprinted the place (and found nothing), carried Marcia off to the morgue, and located the boyfriend. So they told me they were through and left me in the ruins.

Terry Wilson, the 500-year-old police reporter on my paper, and a photographer I didn't know passed the police in the hall, got what they could, and came to see me. They knocked and I let them in, deeply fatigued to see a familiar face. Wilson's little black eyes flitted around the place, taking in a millionth murder. "Jesus, Steve," he murmured when they showed him the mess that bordered a taped human outline on the bed. And for a time that was all anybody said.

But Wilson lingered after the photographer had finished, to ask, "You do it?"

"God, no."

His voice rattled out of him, crept past his old, eroded teeth, flavored by some tone imparted by the long, veinous nose, purpled with drink. "Cops picked up her boyfriend. They seem to think having slugs sprayed all over the place looked like a crime of passion. But, shit, he wouldn't have come on like this. He would've roughed her up, strangled her maybe, but not this sullen banging away from the door."

"What're you getting at, Terry?" I knew, at some level, where he was going. But what paranoia, what egoism, to think someone wanted to hit me. Modesty kept me from understanding him too quickly. It made Wilson an important man in my life: If he hadn't explained my problem to me, they would have picked me off easily, before I even understood they wanted to.

"Has some professional elements and some amateurish ones. Probably a silenced gun, which is kind of uptown. But he doesn't do this a lot; he's only a fair shot or a rattled good shot, not willing to turn the body over and see if the job's really done. Some parts squeamish, some parts mean enough to murder. Nope, the killer just wanted to put as many slugs as he could find into that figure on the bed. The figure was supposed to be you, Steve-o."

"I don't make enemies writing science."

"You want an opinion?"

"Sure."

"You made an enemy."

"Jesus," I said. My flesh moved, knowing he was right. But I couldn't tell him about Cerf, I don't know why.

"What're you working on, Steve?"

"Something about solar flares. Space shuttle. And a NASA, uh, project."

"Christ, that sounds pretty innocent to me." He wandered, letting his eyes rekindle the memory of violence. "Maybe it's mistaken identity." My ego shrank, and I marveled at the selfishness: Some automatic piece of me would rather be a target than a random error. "If I were you, I'd drop out for a time, man. I'll tell Horatio to expect your call. 'Cause, really, they're gonna nail you next time."

After Wilson left I brooded over all this, thinking I had at least a few hours before whoever hit Marcia learned of the error and began a new search for me. They'd have to go on and hit me now, too, take me off the board. But what board, what game, what players? Dunham. I'd screwed a little group of scientific outlaws within NASA to the wall, and they'd talked it over and decided I was expendable. Come on . . . NASA didn't operate like that—it wouldn't know *how* to operate like that.

Except . . . they were the only big enemy I'd made thus far.

Maybe they *would* kill over *Brideshead.* But maybe there was also something else, linked through Cerf perhaps or twisted in with the other two terms; something. So, okay, I decided then, finally and forever, I'd turn the fucking screws down and down until I arrived at whatever central truth or lie set killers loose in my life. In Marcia's. I had to discover the word, the sentence, the paragraph that inspired such easy violence, and open it up to the light.

An hour later I'd cleared what I wanted to keep out of the apartment and booked into a motel way the hell down South Dixie Highway, a motel for failed salesmen and enlisted transients, far from the Miami I thought of as my own. Then I tried to rest; but when I closed my eyes I looked into Marcia's, and the sight jerked me suddenly back to the world, cold and sweaty with fear. I got a couple of hours' sleep before an endless nightmare drew me back, back to an unfamiliar turquoise room and the roar of traffic on the highway.

I got up and cleaned off, cleaned off like Lady Macbeth with a shower, unable to scrub away all the patina of death—got dressed, and walked to a Royal Castle for breakfast. Wilson, moving fast, or maybe writing the story from police reports before he came over, had got the story dropped into the paper. While I ate I read about the murder in a reporter's apartment, the arrested suspect. Wilson didn't speculate about who the victim should have been, either as a favor to me (my big enemy presumably wouldn't want to be detected so early; it would make him angry, stir him up) or because he thought it too soft as news. Probably both.

After breakfast I risked a trip to my bank, where, apprehensive as a robber, I emptied my reporter-sized savings account and got some free travelers checks, then drove back down to Homestead, where I sold the bug on a lot for something like the square root of its retail value. Going back to the motel I took a bus, feeling suddenly very much on top of my situation and more or less in the spirit of the thing. Good-natured prey.

Except I didn't know how to behave and felt that important conventions of being at bay lay outside my experience. I cracked the curtains, then sealed them, not knowing whether one waited blind or waited watching. I tried television, where a barely legible bulletin told me NORAD's new forecast for *Excalibur*'s reentry moved it forward in time and that the derelict was now dropping 3,500 feet per day. I snapped it off. I lay on the bed, thought about taking up cigarettes again, went back through the paper, looked out the window, bored absolutely shitless; and all the time my belief in my situation drained away. Examining my day to its forenoon I felt panicked and silly, stampeded, suspended when I should have been trying to find a path through all the violent shit in my life.

So, for starters, I called Horatio. "Wilson talk to you?" I asked.

"Yeah, Steve." His voice carried unexpected concern, and, unexpectedly, it embarrassed me. "You okay?"

"Sure. I'm . . ."

"Look, I don't really need to know where you are."

"Okay."

"But we oughta talk."

"Did they approve the trips?"

"Yeah, but we need to talk."

"Your place?"

"How about some *plantanos*?"

"When?"

"Seven?"

"Fine."

Horatio acted as if he knew something I didn't. He'd spoken obliquely, as to a bugged phone, and got us off before my call could be traced. *Plantanos* I knew meant we'd meet at a little Cuban place we'd gone to before up on Calle Ocho. As I thought these things, part of me said, Come on, enough paranoia, already. And the rest said, Back on your guard, man.

I considered my moves. It looked like I'd be on the road, and so I decided to lighten my load. I'd brought everything I could carry, which wasn't a hell of a lot but could be refined for lighter travel. I got everything out of the suitcases and put a suit and some chinos and shirts and a windbreaker and essentials like that, and my camera and the little Adler portable, into the smaller one, then refilled the big one with stuff I could live without.

About eleven I took the big suitcase containing all I didn't need and bussed north to Coral Gables, where I rented a little red Plymouth from Japan and headed out to Miami International. I parked within watching distance of the general aviation terminal. One of NASA's pretty Lear jets whistled up to the gate a minute past noon. My first thought was they wouldn't have sent it to pick up a guy they'd killed the night before; but then again maybe they'd read the *Herald*. Maybe they wanted to get me a couple of thousand feet over the ocean and drop me out. I decided not to try them today. They stayed on the ground until two, and I watched them waiting. Then the faceless crew buttoned up the Lear and headed back to Huntsville or wherever. And I drove out to a lonely place near the Government Cut end of Miami Beach and wandered among the old, the surf fishers, and seagulls devouring the afternoon.

2

La Patria sat jammed between a five-and-dime and a boutique on Eighth Avenue, anachronistic and dingy, run by a Cuban couple who were just climbing back into the middle class after some bad years in Miami. Everybody who came over pulled a tour as janitor, or so it seems. Horatio knew them because he ate there often, following the rigid diurnal habit of the older unmarried male. He waited in a back booth and waved at me when I entered. He looked stealthy as a thieving animal. "You're taking this pretty hard," I told him.

He shook his head. "Considering how fast you dropped out of sight, I'd say we both were."

"Touché."

He flagged the waiter, son or cousin or nephew of the owners, and we ordered a couple of St. Pauli Girls. While we waited, Horatio asked, "Any idea what nerve you touched? Or whose?"

My reflex not to talk about *Brideshead* surprised me, but I went with it. "Nope."

"What happened to your Huntsville trip?"

"I put it off."

"Meaning what?"

"Meaning it's more important to find out why Marcia got killed in my apartment."

He shook his head impatiently, an unbeliever.

We waited for the beers to be delivered to the checkered oilcloth. Then he said, "So you don't know who your enemy is, even."

"I think he's big. Governmental, maybe."

"Ours."

"Maybe. Maybe theirs." I could not bring myself to tell him about Cerf either. "I don't know."

"Let's order."

We both got shrimp enchilados and plantano on the side and a second beer.

"You can't stay underground forever," Horatio said through a mouth filled with creole shrimp. "What're your plans?"

"I'm not sure. I need to go push my NASA contacts on this. You know, lie to them, try to fuck them up, get more light on it. Then I need to talk to Sonya Van Deer at Alamo Peak."

"You think it all comes together?"

"I think it's a web. Everything seems to fit somewhere on the web. I don't know if the spider's at NASA headquarters or Huntsville or Alamo Peak or where. But I see its web." I laughed, self-conscious about my predicament. "You know, besides making a boy horny, hiding out breeds paranoia like mold. Yesterday I got out the letters from Danilov, the cosmonaut."

"Died a couple months ago?"

"Yeah."

"He part of your web?"

"I don't know. Maybe. Anyway, they seemed . . ."

"What?" And something in the sound of him, something less than familiar in his face, made me regret mentioning Danilov.

". . . oh, very innocent, given my situation." I veered away.

"I guess they would, at that." Yes, a definite straining quality in the voice, a note that told me he wanted to make something happen. He sensed it, for he gave a kind of shake then and said, "I brought along your travel. We booked you under my name on Eastern Flight seventy-three tonight, to Washington with a change in Atlanta."

"How'd you know?"

"You said you had to go to Washington."

"But I said I'd do that second."

"But tonight you said you wanted Washington first."

"Oh, okay," I said, still wondering why he'd gone ahead and booked me.

"If you want to change these, change them. In fact, it might be a good idea. Then I wouldn't know how to find you. I don't want to know."

"No, they're fine. You just anticipated me, is all."

"I tried to think where I'd want to go in your shoes."

"Sure."

"Then we have this open round trip from Washington to Albuquerque and Alamogordo, which you can also use to get back to Miami. And some dough." He added ten folded hundred-dollar bills to the tickets.

"They spared nothing."

"The paper looks after its own."

"Who else knows about this?" I asked.

"Our fuehrer. Terry Wilson knows you got a problem. Me. That's it. Word in the city room is you're on leave. I imagine there'll be some leakage to the effect you're on some strange assignment. But nobody knows your itinerary but you."

"You really came through, sir."

"Look, Steve," and I heard the tonal shift of a salesman in there, "you're in exactly the same situation as a reporter who's gone up against the mob. We've put a bunch of people in jail, and we've gone through the same kind of drill protecting the reporters who had the action then. We're a little more expensive on you because we can't tell yet how big your enemy is. It looks like the world."

"So it does."

We talked. We kept it friendly. But my paranoia began working on this old relationship too, seeing faint changes in manner, in look, reading vibes . . . I tried to shake away the distrust, wanting to trust *someone,* and could not. I don't know whether Horatio sensed this or not. Toward the end he had a melancholy diffidence I'd never seen in him before. We left together, walked to my car, and I handed over the big suitcase full of my life to keep for me and helped him carry it across Eighth to his silver LTD. He wished me well. We said good-bye. I watched him drive away. Then, nervous and exposed, I began brushing dirt across my track.

The first thing I did was drive back to the car rental station in the Gables and exchange the red subcompact for a green Toyota. Then I went by my motel and called the little old lady named Muriel (or, sometimes Madame Defarge) who handled travel money. "Hi," I told her, "it's Steve Borg."

"Hello, Steve," she replied, wondering who Steve Borg was.

"Sorry to call you at home, Muriel, but I had a couple of questions on Horatio's travel to Washington."

"What travel is that, Steve?"

"I thought he was booked to Washington tonight."

"If he was, it wasn't through me. Of course, anybody can get a ticket anywhere. It's a free country." She said this in a resentful voice that told me she would forever hate anyone at the paper who got airline tickets anywhere else.

"He was concerned that his travel advance wouldn't cover the trip."

"I don't know anything about it, Steve. He didn't get an advance from me. Are you sure he's taking a trip?"

"Muriel, I probably got the whole thing wrong. Sorry to trouble you."

"No trouble," she said, meaning it had been. "Good-bye."

I put the phone down, feeling sick. But only for a moment. My instincts were developing fast, a generation a night. A day earlier I wouldn't have checked with Muriel. Twelve hours earlier I would have fled. As it was, I did the whole bit for whomever they'd set to watch me. At nine-fifteen I turned in my Toyota at Miami International, checked in at Eastern with my single bag as a carry-on piece, and went down the concourse to my gate, nervous about people clattering up behind me, appearing suddenly out of rest-room doors; I realized that I'd come to live in a world where conspiracy shone in every pair of eyes, and every pair of eyes looked at me coldly, destructively. Remember, if you're wrong, you're paranoid, I thought, forcing myself through the sea of hostile strangers. When they opened the stand I got my seat assigned. I even boarded at our first call, boarded with the bare handful of other souls sharing this short red-eye flight to Atlanta and D.C., found my place behind the DC-9's little wing, and settled in.

But then, a couple of minutes before flight time, I wheezed up to the attendant and whispered to her, "Pace . . . maker . . ." and staggered off the plane with my bag, back to the concourse, joining the river of people that flowed toward the terminal, then took the escalator down to rent another car.

Reequipped with a red Gran Prix, I boomed out to Hialeah, which was no more my part of town than Homestead was, picked up a quart of beer and a novel about the thirtieth century, and drove another half mile to a Cuban motel. The sleepy, sweaty little man in a tank top sold me a sweet-smelling, rose-walled room, where I opened my beer and turned on the televison. I'd come up in the world—the picture was in color (running to infrared visions) and the people were the right size.

While whatever it was—the tail end of a Richard Arlen aviation adventure, I think—flickered across the room, I thought about the enemy and wondered how he, they, would have done it: a hatpin to the base of my young brain, the sudden lethal roistering into one of the lavatories, a poisoned snack? And the pilot and first officer and cabin attendants and battalion of passengers (federal employees all) would stand around applauding when I lay in the aisle, quieted at last. Such fancies and the Arlen film were interrupted by a sad-faced, sincere man who told us Eastern Flight 73 had exploded over the water east of Jacksonville, killing twenty-five.

Actually, twenty-four.

I decided not to call Horatio again.

3

The fireball surging up the aisle drove me out of sleep, returned me to the world spiritless and frightened, depressed by a night of very bad dreams that had finally restored me to the Eastern DC–9, to my seat behind the wing, and kept me there, silently knowing that, in an hour, we must disintegrate in flames, fall endlessly toward the dark sea . . .

Even awake my mind watched the fuselage rupture, the flame, the bodies spilling seaward.

So by five I was reluctant to close my eyes again. For a time I lay around, watching the rose sky of the ceiling begin to color the darkness, listening to the traffic hiss down streets wet with early morning rain, the air conditioner struggling to breathe all that humidity, the birds just commencing their morning fuss; and, finally, with my realities somewhat composed, I got up and began putting myself together for another day of being prey. Long shower, close shave, chinos, Wallabees, and a knit shirt and windbreaker—clothes to flee in.

On the television news, the world had its usual problems. Some international misunderstandings. Retaliatory bombings in the Middle East. Inflation, up. Dollar, down. An aeronautical tragedy over the Atlantic off Jacksonville (I shuddered involuntarily), the victims' names withheld pending notification . . .

I wondered how long I could stay dead. They'd have backtracked to Horatio, found him alive, discovered I'd used his ticket. They'd call my mother in Illinois, frighten her with the news; she had to be prepared, I'd tell her the CIA recruited me . . . something.

But what did I have that was worth twenty-four lives? Or, rather, worth an airplane carrying x people? Shit, they could have killed thirty, or fifty, or a hundred. And this escalation made me think, Ah, paranoia: The plane blew up. With you or without you, man, it would have exploded.

Something stared at me from the television screen, and it took me a minute to realize what it was: the sun, the big gaseous sphere mottled as an orange in the red line of hydrogen, diaphanous, distant, exotic, and looking meaner than hell. The meanness resided in a bright region spreading over the upper left-hand quadrant of the solar disk—the northeast quadrant, in the reversed sense used by solar forecasters. You could see a cluster of large spots in the middle of the dazzlingly bright plage, and while I watched, the region near one of the sunspots erupted, flashed bright, a great bomb that rippled the wrinkled surface. ". . . Awesome spectacle of the sun," the anchor was saying, and one had to agree. Awesome was the word. H-alpha photos of active sunspot regions crossed my desk all the time, and I'd never seen anything of this size—not even in August 1972. I loved it. I could have watched our stormy star all day, like a professional soldier watching war. It lingered on my memory even after the anchor's earnest face replaced it. "This angry sun is complicating the task of estimating when space shuttle *Excalibur* will reenter the atmosphere. The North American Air Defense Command says present forecasts show the hulk reentering over the Pacific Ocean in about ten days and report that *Excalibur*'s orbit is losing nearly a mile a day at the present time." Then the juggernaut of news rolled on to something more predictable.

I called my mother, getting her small voice sleepy and puzzled from Illinois. I told her who I was and talked a little about this and that to get her awake and up to speed. Then I said, "Look, Ma, there's been a little misunderstanding."

"Don't worry about it, son."

"I don't mean between us. An airliner blew up last night. I was supposed to be on it." She began to cry softly. "But I wasn't. It was just a mistake." The crying hesitated, listening. "It's just that somebody may call you to tell you I was killed on the plane." The crying resumed. "And I wanted you to know I'm perfectly fine."

"Oh, I'm so glad, Steven."

"Ma, it would help if, when they call, you act as though you think I'm dead, okay?"

"I wouldn't want to fib, son."

"No problem. Never mind."

"Are you in some trouble?"

"No, not at all. I'm doing something confidential, uh, with the government."

"Is it dangerous?"

"Not at all."

"I'll tell them you're dead."

"Okay, Ma, appreciate it."

"Are you in Miami?"

"Yes, Ma."

"Steven."

"Yes?"

"You got a letter here that I haven't had a chance to forward."

"From where?"

"Hold on just a moment." The phone went hollow while she padded off into the house, then returned. "It's from Geneva, Switzerland."

"Could you read it to me, Ma?"

"On the telephone?"

"Yes, please."

"Well, all right." She was quiet, opening the envelope. Then she said, relieved, "It's short."

"Good. Please read it."

"All right, Steven." And she read:

Dear Friend Steven,

   Here is a springtime New Year's greeting for you, and a space poem to read along with my other letters.

KIEV CENTRE

The great star trembles,
Ready to fall,
The Godfoot.
The people watch from their shadows,
Readying rockets for
Cosmonaut sappers
To keep the star from
Kiev Centre.

Remember some of my words, although, sending a poem to a writer
may be extreme, as mutual friend John Chester might say. A very
good year to you, my friend, and good-bye from

Vladimir Sergeevich Danilov

4

We talked awkwardly for a paragraph or two after she read me Danilov's letter, and then I had her do it again while I wrote it down, and then we did a little more talking and finally it broke apart, which was how we ended most of our telephone conversations. I never knew how much between us was blood and how much habit. For a time I turned the poem over and over in my mind, trying to fit it against my puzzle, lacking the skill; but I knew it was Danilov's key.

I checked out of the motel and took myself to breakfast at a Cuban place across from the Hialeah track. And there, while munching and dunking and searching for further news of me in the paper (and finding none), I fretted over my Next Move. Washington still looked good. I had some probing questions for Dunham, like, why'd you have Marcia hit? But everything seemed to be so goddamned wired together I didn't know right away how to get there undetected. And, fixed on Dunham and my travel problems, I neglected John Chester.

The answer droned at me outside the restaurant, rumbled down from the hot, pale light that begins the summer mornings in Miami. A tiny airplane drifted down its invisible wire, its wheels hanging down gracelessly, its wings rocking in slight currents. I watched it turn north, fly nearly to the horizon, and settle somewhere. Opa Locka.

So I followed it in the crimson Gran Prix, jogging a little to the east to get back to LeJeune Road, and finally entered the compound of concrete and grass and hangars that composed this hive of airplanes, middle sized to tiny. There was a Coast Guard operation near where I entered the airport grounds, a busy squadron of amphibs and choppers dressed in orange and white and some big operators in the large hangars over by the tower. These looked more organization-minded than I wanted, and so I shopped around the smaller stuccoed buildings on the field, the flight schools and charter services, until I was drawn by a flag-colored sign between golden wings that said:

RUDD AIR SERVICE
Rental * Charter * Instruction
"Ruddy good aviation!"

I guess I half-expected to find, beyond the busted screen door and old naugahyde sofas and a magazine rack and the ubiquitous counter filled with circular computers, manuals, and sunglasses, a British pilot, fiftyish, wearing a Spitfire suit of fleece and leather, ready to speed me off to Washington in something pretty small but pretty hot. As it was I found a small, clean-limbed brunette with her hair in a pageboy cut, a face well formed and classy in kind of an English way, pale and full-lipped, breasts middle sized and free beneath a poplin shirt; and in the ocean color of the eyes, a seriousness that said there had never been a man pass this way who could give her any shit. But . . . friendly. She gave me a serious look and said, "Hi," in a voice I found melodic.

"Hi," I replied, unexpectedly warmed by the sound of a neutral human.

"Can I help you?"

"I need to go to Washington."

"D.C.?"

"Yep. I need to know how soon and how much."

"You tried National? Takes a couple of hours. Dinner, drinks. Pretty girls."

"Come on."

"I'd use the Rug . . ."

"The Rug?"

"The Cardinal RG, for retractable gear. It costs seventy-five dollars an hour with a pilot who flies back solo, fifty-five dollars an hour where I make the round trip with you. Takes about six hours, one way."

"That'd be right around four hundred fifty bucks."

"National does it for about a sixth of that."

"You sound like a stockholder."

"I'm on their flight engineer list. Maybe if they make some money they'll hire me on."

"The heart has its reasons."

"As the man said."

"Who's Rudd?" I wanted to know.

"I am."

"Who'd fly me to Washington?"

"I would."

"I'm, uh, not real experienced in small airplanes."

"You should take National."

"I can't."

"How come?"

"Without going into a lot of detail . . ."

"Okay."

". . . I have a problem. But it's not with the cops. Nothing illegal. It's just important to me to keep a low profile right now."

"I guess that's all I really need to know. How soon can you leave?"

"I'd like to go to the bathroom first."

"You do that. I'll get us ready."

When I got back she was just finishing filing her flight plan by phone. "There's some weather between here and D.C. We ought to get there all right, but I'm not sure I'll get back today."

"That'd make kind of a long day."

"You're right." Then, "I'll be wanting a couple of hundred in advance."

"Sure." I got out Horatio's money envelope and pulled out five hundreds. "If there's any change I can get it in D.C."

"Okay."

She got a backpack, which I guessed held her overnight things, and we headed out, with a stop at my rented Pontiac to get my bag, then through an alley between hangars to a ramp full of little airplanes, which all looked pretty much the same to me. Hers was mauve and vermillion and white, a streamlined machine that looked as if it was flying when it sat on its thin bowed legs on the concrete. I helped her untie it, and she opened it up, took the gust lock out of the controls and walked around her plane, drained fuel from its sumps, poked and prodded and wiggled it for airworthiness.

When we were strapping ourselves into the front seats I said, "In case you feel the need to call out to someone, my name's Steve."

She laughed. "Mine's Pam." Being in an airplane softened her.

"Ruddy good."

"My dad's slogan."

"I sort of expected to see someone's father in there."

"He's dead." She frowned, then went to her piloting. The machine whined, shuddered, came to life, the incomprehensible chatter from the radio filled the cockpit. "Cardinal three-four-five-one-six ready to taxi from Rudd to the active with Bravo," she told the tower. They responded, but all I could understand was our airplane number. We taxied out, ran the engine up, and took our place in line to leave Opa Locka toward the east.

Then we were off, the wheels hissed up into the fuselage. I watched the world drop away, watched the ramp go by where we had begun this flight, saw Rudd Air Service's little buildings, saw a pair of black sedans crowding my big red Pontiac.

I thought I'd run farther ahead of them than that.

5

She steered us along the coast, drifting a mile or two offshore as we climbed to cruising altitude, which turned out to be nine thousand feet. The machine preoccupied her; she listened to it, fiddled with the mixture and throttle. But, once cruising on auto-pilot, she turned to me and said over the drumming of the engine, "I couldn't help but notice a bunch of black sedans by your car."

I nodded. "I saw them."

"They mean whoever wants you knows you flew out with Pam Rudd."

"I guess they do."

"What's that do to me?"

"I don't know."

"You don't." The serious eyes flicked at the instruments, scanned the sky around us, and returned to me. "Maybe you need to tell me your problem."

"It isn't with the law or the mob, okay? Maybe it's paranoia."

"Okay."

"I'm a reporter."

"Good."

"I think they're trying to kill me over a story." *They* had a crazy sound I didn't like.

"*They* kill anybody yet?" She gave the pronoun some inflection, so I'd know she heard the insanity in it too.

I shook my head, turned to watch the altocumulus clouds,

which hover perpetually over middle Florida, walk by between us and the sea.

"That mean no or you don't want to go on?"

"It means it sounds, it feels, paranoid as hell."

"Still, if we're going to D.C. together, best you share it with me."

"Meaning we're not going if I don't."

"Maybe. Tell me."

"Couldn't I just hijack you?"

"You could try; but don't." She did her instrument scan and looked at me. "I'm a very tough broad. Tell me your problem."

"Somebody shot and killed a lady friend sleeping where I usually sleep."

"Jealous husband?"

"I was ticketed on the Eastern plane that blew up last night. They thought I was on it."

"Jesus! *That's* kind of far to go."

"You're right. For all I know, it's coincidental."

"For all you know." Her eyes held something like pity for me.

"I thought I had a longer head start. Otherwise I wouldn't have involved you."

"And then again, you probably would've. Don't worry about it, shuggie. I guess I know more than I need to. Don't tell me the rest."

In a small plane you punctuate your talk with the silence that waits behind the beating of the engine. We let ourselves go quiet. I watched the sea and its tiny ships trailing tiny wakes, streets of small low clouds, a sudden airplane skidding across our field of view. She flew a course halfway between a straight line to Washington and the westward bow of the coast, adjusting her radios to monitor our passage northward. Voices of pilots and briefers came over the Flight Watch channel, dismembered voices scattered over the southeastern states. Sometimes we could hear the briefer, sometimes the pilot, occasionally both. And from these conversations of all those severed heads, it came clear that the good weather would be with us only to the northern border of South Carolina.

"That mean we have to set down somewhere?" I asked.

She shook her head. "We'll intersect the coast at Charleston, refuel there, and go on IFR."

"IFR?"

"On instruments."

"I thought only big planes did that."

"Nope. Little ones do just fine."

Silence again. She scanned, adjusted, flew. I watched her profile, the profile of an English girl, woman, fine of nose, fine of mouth and chin, intelligent. Her long hands moved expertly in their small adjustments of trim and power. And, through the cockpit odor of the plane (people perspire a lot in planes) came her soapy smell. It made a contented man of me, and I relaxed into my seat, ready to sleep.

Beyond her profile the low green blur of the Carolina coastline moved toward us, the coastal plain all tattered with inlets and estuaries. The horseshoe-shaped estuary around Beaufort slid past, and Pam pulled back the power and the rpm to begin a gradual descent.

I didn't see the Phantom. I just saw a split-second tightening about Pam's eyes, the twist of her shoulder as she went for the throttle, tightened her grip on the wheel. The jet went by us unbelievably close, unbelievably fast, loud, lost as suddenly as it came in a dark cloud of exhaust, while we rolled sickeningly in its turbulent wake. It was like being brushed by a large shark in shallow water, frightening beyond anticipation or belief. Pam moved swiftly and shut down the engine, flew the machine through a split-S like a glider, and turned everything on again. The large, gentle maneuver put us on the deck, and she took us down still farther, until we skimmed the waves along the dune-contoured beach. I thought we probably left a wake behind us. Ahead of us we saw the Phantom angle down, then level out on a collision course, a dark streamlined dot against its smoke cloud. Pam banked suddenly northwest, following a brown, sluggish river; then, as the Phantom adjusted its path to meet us, she turned back to the northeast, somewhat slower, following the bank that ran between grassy hills and low trees, staying lower than the treetops. The Phantom came over us very fast, very close, and again we rocked in its turbulence; Pam climbed behind the jet, so that we got jostled, but the descending vortices from the Phantom didn't spin us into the river. She continued her climb, following the river back to the north. The jet broke off. Soon it was just another vapor trail, moving across the dome of sky.

Abruptly Pam was on the radio; we were over a small airport with a bunch of little planes and, in our turn, lined up with the north-south runway and landed. When we were taxiing back toward the nose hangars, she shook her head but said nothing. Her fingers trembled faintly, less from fear I supposed than from an overdose of adrenalin, which I hoped was the reason for my own poorly concealed case of the shakes.

"Where are we?" I asked, shifting our subject.

"John's Island, south of Charleston. We'll wee-wee and get some gas and be on our way."

"Maybe I better go the rest of the way alone."

"I don't see the need of that."

She taxied us up to the Phillips pump and shut the Cardinal down. A line boy wearing a John's Island T-shirt, with isolated black hairs on arms and face and a lot of acne, came out and she told him to top it off. Before she got out, she said to me, "That kind of thing happens all the time around here with military jets. Those boys need a target, is all. Don't go thinking it was meant for you."

"Fine."

"I mean, pretty soon you begin to think every damned thing that happens is meant for you, and in a way that shapes what happens to you."

"You're right." Steve Borg had become a self-fulfilling prophecy. But, see, I knew, and she knew, that the jet had come from my big fucking enemy, the BFE, who now was also hers.

6

We clipped a few thin clouds on our way back to nine thousand climbing out past Charleston. Then, settled into a steady cruise, we could make out the band of ugly weather that separated us from Washington. A layer of high cirrus overhead seemed to taper to the horizon, where it met a thick, roiled floor of low clouds that vanished in the haze below; and there, with occasional artillerylike flashes of lightning, the weather began. Pam turned on the cockpit lights and pushed the visual navigation charts over to me, opening a smaller chart, that, to my eye, seemed all purple lines and abbreviated names. Our eyes met and she grinned for me. "Really, little planes fly on instruments all the time. I'm going to go on and file IFR to D.C. now. Pardon me while I go into isolation. If you want to listen, there's a headset in the glove compartment there." She slid a big green headset with a boom mike over her brown pageboy, which, I noticed, ran to thin streaks of gold; British blond.

For a time I stayed white knuckled and ignorant, watching us begin to hurry toward the center of all this dirty weather, as though we rode a raft captured by the rim of a whirlpool, drawn irresistibly toward the watery funnel. The air roughened, the strutless wings on the Cardinal went *creak* and *crack*. Pam pulled back the power some, wriggled around in her seat, getting ready; then, suddenly, we flew into the maelstrom of cloud and wind and giant raindrops.

Looking outside I could see our airplane and that was about all. Rain, and sometimes rain mixed with the mushy ice called graupel, hosed the windscreen, crawled back along the side windows, building and bursting along the riveted waterways of the wing's lower surface. Lightning uncoiled like bright streamers, jabbing at a vanishing point below. The air thumped at the thin skin of the Cardinal. I closed my eyes and tried to let the passage happen without me. That failing, I fumbled in the glove compartment and brought out the less elaborate headset that consisted of a bug for one ear and a tiny mike suspended at lip level, slid it on, and looked for a jack to plug it into. Pam noticed, pointed out the jack, and watched intermittently while I got plugged in. "Not much on right now," she said, leaning close enough that I could hear her. "It'll pick up closer to Washington."

"Where are we now?"

"Just passed Florence VOR." She tapped a purple triangle on her chart, which showed an abstract coastline, lakes, and purple and brown lines going everywhere and nowhere. "Little under four hundred miles to go. Just under three hours."

"That's a long time in the rain."

"We'll be in and out all the way up there."

"I admire your stamina."

"Thank you, sir." And she returned to the partnership she'd formed with the autopilot, adjusting, handling the radio, studying the booklets and charts in her lap, while the machine kept the wings level in the storm.

Now and then a southern voice on the radio would speak to someone else in the weather, in the sky, and a voice would come back, the calm leading the calm. Occasionally the voice would say, "Cardinal three-four-five-one-six, Jacksonville," and Pam would reply, and he would ask our position or give us weather or shift our arrival time at Washington National. I thought he talked to us a lot, but she didn't seem concerned.

After what seemed an eternity of flight, we came to a stretch of broken clouds at our altitude, tumbling down to soft bases well below us, rising to the gray layer overhead. Ugly weather; it looked like Miami in winter to me. I made myself relax and noticed she did the same, getting in shape for the next bull, which hid in the raggedy clouds we sliced. And then we were back in the half-light of weather and water, and the shaking resumed in earnest.

She got busy again. I watched the atmospheric madness outside my window.

The southern voice said, "Cardinal three-four-five-one-six, Jacksonville."

"Five one six," Pam replied.

"Five one six, go to Washington Center, one three four point three, and good day, ma'am."

"Five one six, thank you," she said, twisting the frequency selector on her number-one radio. "Washington Center, Cardinal three-four-five-one-six with you at nine thousand."

"Roger, uh, five one six, we have you five south of Brooke VOR. Say your airspeed."

"Five one six, we're making one three zero knots."

"Roger, five one six, one three zero. Stand by."

I listened like an occidental listening to Chinese. It had a friendly sound, though, and the easy familiarity with which these strangers chatted on their radios slowed my heart rate when a big atmospheric hand would seem to hold and shake the Cardinal, then release it a minute or two before grabbing it again.

The voices resumed, Washington clearing us here, Pam reporting us there, Washington letting us descend near Dulles, Pam acting. We began to ease down through the cloud, into the early afternoon half-light. I'd become almost familiar with the instrument panel. The altimeter and airspeed indicator and vertical speed indicator had entered my passenger's scan. Also the distance-measuring equipment, which now counted down the miles to Dulles, or somewhere. The ground voice told her to contact approach control at Washington National, which she did, getting a new voice, a black voice I decided, and let us be worked in closer to our crowded destination. Pam echoed the instructions, keeping busy. Outside all I could see was water streaking the Plexiglas windows, forming tiny rapids along the wing, steaming in ragged gray cloud; we crossed no narrow breaks now, and the gray-green smear of ground we'd sometimes seen lay invisible below the semidarkness that enveloped us. The air continued rough, but I, like a new equestrian, had begun to post with the waves of air that hit us, threw us upward, pushed us down, so that I flew with flesh-colored knuckles once more.

"Five one six, Washington approach."

A new voice. Pam glanced at me, frowned. I looked away, knowing nothing of air-traffic conventions.

"Five one six, Washington, do you read?"

"Five one six."

"Five one six, we're backing up at DCA. How's your fuel?"

"Five one six has a couple hours," Pam replied, still frowning.

"Five one six, okay, ma'am, turn to three three zero and say your altitude."

"Five thousand for five one six," she said, turning to the northwest.

"Okay, five one six, you can come down to three thousand."

"Five one six out of five for three." She pulled back the power slightly, and we began a shallow dive we couldn't feel kinesthetically. Only the unwinding of the altimeter and the vertical-speed indicator told us we were dropping earthward through the weather. Pam changed frequencies on the navigation side of one radio. "Let me see those sectionals, Steve," she told me in a mildly distressed voice. I passed her the charts she'd given me to hold. She unfolded one on her lap under the booklet of instrument-approach diagrams. Then she took out a felt-tip pen and marked a heavy *x* for one position and drew a line up to the northwest. "They're talking, not flying," she said to nobody in particular.

"Five one six, turn to zero five zero, maintain three thousand."

"Five one six to zero five zero," Pam replied.

He droned on, calling other aircraft among the legion of planes converging on Washington in cloud. Pam scanned her instruments and the flat gray expanse surrounding us nervously. If she'd been an animal her ears would have been standing up, moving around, trying to identify the vague trouble she barely sensed, find the hunters in the forest. Seeing her put a hand of fear around my heart, too. She glanced at me, read my feelings, and shook her head. "It's okay," she said and again changed the nav frequency and marked her map.

"Five one six, descend to two thousand and turn to zero niner zero."

She echoed. The DME counted down the miles. "Is that to Washington National?" I asked.

Pam nodded. It showed us ten nautical miles away. She glanced at the approach diagram and then at the chart. Our shallow dive continued, the altimeter wound down toward the two. And she began to lean forward, hold the wheel with more authority; her right hand touched the throttle, and her scan included a look straight down through her side window, a vigil that clearly longed to see the Earth, which scared me further. I matched her tension, but had nothing to do with it except to let my stomach ache.

"Five one six, turn to one eight zero and descend to one thousand; contact the tower on one one niner point one, good day."

She repeated the litany, then extended the landing gear and added a few degrees of flap, getting ready to return to Earth. Our dive continued toward the one on the altimeter. Below us we could begin to see the low, flat structures and trees of the city, strung across its rounded hills; but ahead of us the gray wall persisted. "Washington tower," she said on the new frequency, "Cardinal three-four-five-one-six seven northeast on final for one eight."

"Cardinal three-four-five-one-six, Washington tower, say your airspeed and altitude."

"Five one six, one one zero knots at one thous . . . *Jesus!*" She saw the urgent strobing of the television towers that rose suddenly half a second ahead of us, rolled the Cardinal hard to the right, and, on knife edge, pushed hard on the throttle and dived the airplane, picking up speed. Time suspended. The town rushed by a couple of hundred feet below us, great trees and oblong apartment buildings, rain slick, car-choked streets in the trapezoidal road patterns of that city, then the low hills of Georgetown running down to the Potomac, where she turned back to the northwest no more than a hundred feet above the water, retracted the gear and flaps, turned off her transponder and outside lights, and headed upriver. As we mounted the Potomac we could hear the bereft controller, "Five one six, do you read? Five one six?" The monotone gave us nothing. You want a requiem, don't ask the FAA. "Five one six, do you read?"

We read him, but that would have to be our secret. Pam steered us up the Potomac, whose banks rose above us on either side. We suspended between the gray water of the river and the gray weather overhead, charging through the pale-colored afternoon. People along the banks watched our passage, some waved. It was an exhilarating flight, and at last, when we rose nearly to the cloud bases in a soaring turn, I shivered with excitement. "For a moment I thought we were swimming upriver to spawn."

She gave me a long, sideways look, and grinned. "Know what happens after we spawn, Steve?"

"I try not to think about the dark side."

"Yeah, I noticed that." And she laughed.

Now she turned north until we crossed the interstate heading out toward Frederick, then brought the plane about and searched the rolling patchwork that makes so much of Maryland look the same from the air. We were in the pattern before I picked out the narrow runway at Gaithersburg, and she was telling the other traffic what she intended, using a phony airplane number on the radio. In a moment we were down, inclined to kiss the Earth—or someone.

Taxiing toward the little terminal she said, "Steve, you sho' God got me involved."

"I only know English. You have to tell me what happened."

"They vectored us around and around until we were just lined up with those towers and below them. And I would've gone along if they hadn't changed controllers in midcontrol. I'm so goddamned paranoid after spending the day in your company that I noticed."

"You're only paranoid if you're wrong, Pam."

"That's what I keep telling myself, hon." But when she'd parked where the line boy told us and got the Cardinal shut down, she leaned back into her seat, limp and tired, smiling like a woman well laid. I leaned over and pecked her on one soap-scented cheek and said, "You done good."

She whirled, I guess to remind me what a toughie she was. But somebody had nearly killed us, and she'd scraped us loose. Life looked pretty good to both of us at that moment, so it was natural that we should have only long, deep looks for one another and spend a minute or two in friendly embrace; and for the line boy, whose eyes were as clear of conspiracy as a baby's, to shuffle back to his gas truck and leave us in our metal cocoon, where I got to feel how her rugged little back fit within my arms, gauge the softness of her hair, touch the wonderful curve where her waist went to hip and thigh, stroke away the death that had nearly taken us.

7

Together we tied down the Cardinal and got our luggage, unable not to touch, diffident when we did. The day had left us bound. At the terminal she let them run off a credit-card ticket for fuel while I rented a car that turned out to be a blue Fairmont. We drove off into the winding roads and farmlands, still hot and green with summer and late afternoon, and found the Holiday Inn, sterile, familiar, somehow beyond conspiracy; you wouldn't expect a poisoned Big Mac, either. And there, standing on the same carpet before the same desk and perhaps the same pimpled clerk, I faltered, looked to Pam for reassurance, received her nod, and signed us up for a fifty-dollar double.

The room smelled new, the fixtures freshly caulked. Pam ran back the curtain so we could see the afternoon preparing for its hazy end. I lay down on one of the big beds with my arms crossed behind my head and watched her, watched the fine, long-legged moves. Her face had gone gentle, the aviator's crow's-feet softened by the room's softer light. Something in the fear and near misses of our day had left her focused inward, smiling at something within. A pretty sight, red lipped and English, and I realized with some surprise that she'd produced in me my first sexual thought since finding Marcia. I said, "I really like the look of you."

She flinched slightly, surprised from privacy, and smiled. She came over and sat down next to me, and I took her hands between mine. "Hell of a day," I told her.

"Wasn't it?" Then, after a moment's reflection, "Hard to believe how bad they want to kill you."

"Us."

"Oh, they don't care about me at all. They just want you. Who is it anyway?"

"Don't know. Tonight we may find out."

She put her head on my chest, and I wrapped an arm around her. We both shivered involuntarily, needing the contact. "What's your plan?" she asked.

"I thought I'd help you take off your clothes."

"Mm," she said.

I fiddled with her buttons, slowly peeled her down to a beautiful slender body, pale as cream but faintly touched with Miami sunshine, fine breasted, the neck longish, rising from shoulders that were broad for a lady and straight as a boy's; but the narrow waist was most womanly, spreading suddenly into a lovely curve of hip, and these tapering into slender skier's legs. "Don't look much like a pilot now, miss."

"You don't look much like a reporter," she replied as I stepped out of my pile of clothing. "Something like an elephant, but not much like a reporter."

But up closer her ocean-colored eyes were deep and somehow sad, even with a smile around them, and I thought, for a tough cunt, you're pretty vulnerable. And then we were off . . .

We did well together, we fit, sharing textures and tastes and rhythms; most of the sadness drained from her eyes. She lay against me while we watched the pale red sun drop through the Maryland haze and beyond the time-rounded hills off to the west. She said, "Don't look much like an elephant now."

"Nope. He dreams."

"To repeat, what's your plan."

"Need to see if I can handle simple chores. Go to bathroom. Take nourishment. Use phone book."

"In your weakened condition?"

"A gigantic loss of bindu. Vital bodily fluids."

"A good yoga could draw it back in."

"Can I try?"

She laughed. "He looks pretty sleepy, hon. Not to mention pale and blue."

"Want to hear Plan X?"

"Sure."

"The reason I'm in the soup is I picked open something NASA wanted kept quiet."

"You think NASA . . . ?"

"I didn't used to, but who knows? So there's a NASA guy, Les Dunham, I need to see. I need to surprise him, scare him maybe, find out what they're doing to me. To us."

"Us," she echoed.

"He's over in Virginia."

"Want me to go?"

I shook my head. "If it sours I'd rather have you back here."

"They'll still come after me."

"Yeah, but . . ." I peered into the eyes, which had gone serious and sad again. "I'm real new at this stuff, Pam. I sort of need to do it out of sight. Wait'll I get better, okay?"

"How'll I know if it goes sour?"

"Good question. I guess if I'm not back by midnight, you should fly on out of here. Okay?"

"Sure, okay." But the look persisted.

"I know they'll still come after you. I don't know what to do about that."

"Me neither."

"Unless the whole thing's opened up. Then they'll leave us alone."

"They." She gave her head an angry shake and got up quickly like a dancer. "They. Jesus Christ." Her body glowed in the half-light as she crossed the room and knelt by her backpack. When she stood up she had a gun.

For a time she stood with her weight on one long leg, the snub-nosed revolver gleaming at me. I couldn't watch her. There seemed no boundaries to the scope of conspiracy and betrayal. When she came near I leapt at her, leapt for the gun, the move of a despairing man, sluggish and poorly sprung; and she twisted easily away from my lunge, then leaned toward me, understanding where I was, saying, "No, babe, no. Here, take it. Take it," until I comprehended. And then she lay protectively over me, saying softly, "Not me, not me, hon, really, not me."

"Sorry," I muttered, ashamed, still drawing back from her. "The gun . . ."

"I thought you better take some iron." She lay the gleaming little gun next to my hand. "Know how to use it?" I nodded. "It'll get you back here before any midnight, babe."

"Thanks."

"We'll feel better after a bath."

8

I missed Pam as soon as I left the motel and missed her more with increased distance from Gaithersburg, so that it took me nearly to the Potomac to begin getting my act together. The area fled by, vaguely familiar from my army days but heavily built up, camouflaged by progress. In an hour I entered the brick maze of northern Virginia, all trees and red apartment buildings and white colonials row upon row. And an hour after that I'd managed, with the help of the rental car's maps and a couple of gas-station attendants, to navigate into Les Dunham's neighborhood.

The house was one of those tall, thin, light-brick colonials on a narrow lot, expensive but not too expensive, a way of using unusable trapezoids and triangles of land, a place purchased at forty, worth a hundred twenty, its value distended with the Washington bubble. I parked across the elm-lined street, opened the window so the wet night air could creep in and remove some of the chill. For it had come to me that a tough-guy approach was something I didn't know shit about except what I'd seen in the movies. In the real world, the only tough guys I'd seen were psychopathic punks, too dumb to understand that what they felt was fear. There were no good tough guys in my experience. And then I thought about the silenced shots wasting Marcia; the two dozen souls on that Eastern flight, sent casually on a fearful fall into oblivion; of the conspiracy of death that had stalked Pam and me from Opa Locka. And I thought: Stay mad. Make him tell what he knows. If

Dunham set all this in motion, shoot him. That went too far, and I amended it: No, just keep his death in mind as a real possibility. Just a possibility.

Thus fortified, I got out and crossed to the Dunham house, the revolver palmed in a nervous, sweaty hand in my windbreaker pocket, my heart thumping the way it did when, with trembling hands, I fanned my cards and saw four aces. Not fear, you see, but *great* excitement.

A weedy cultivated rectangle near the front steps marked someone's effort to get a garden started in the scraped clay of the shallow yard, and some tired roses climbed halfheartedly along trellises bordering a glossy white and yellow door. I rang. The bells echoed through the place. Footsteps. A blonde girl about ten opened the door and looked at me, brown eyed, somber—Dunham's pretty daughter. "Hi," I said. "Your dad in?"

"Are you a friend of his?"

"Yes."

She let me into the narrow hall, from which stairs went up a floor and doors opened onto living and dining rooms and a kind of den. The girl called, "Daddy, it's someone for you," and left me there. Then Dunham came out of the den.

He stopped when he saw me. I think it took a moment for him to recognize me outside my working context, so far from my own turf; to Dunham I was mainly a telephone voice heard in his big office at NASA headquarters, not this vaguely familiar ghost in his foyer. I tried to look into his soul to see whether he wondered why I wasn't dead, but nothing in the little man's wrinkled Irish monkey face said that. Just the surprise one would expect, then curiosity. "Steve . . .?" He grinned and came over, extended his hand. I turned loose of the revolver and shook the proffered paw, then returned mine to its heavy pocket.

"Needed to talk to you, Les," I said, still nervous, afraid he'd do something sudden that would make me shoot him off a reflex of apprehension and fear.

"Didn't know you were in town."

"I wasn't."

He led me into the little den from which he'd emerged, where a small desk deep in papers crouched in a pool of fluorescent light that glowed like a pale fire in a canyon of books. "Sit down. Want some coffee?"

"No thanks."

"Mind if I do?"

"We'd better talk."

"Cigarette?" I shook my head. "Mind if I smoke?" He was scared, and, noticing his fear, I began to close his case.

I laughed as confidence returned. "Mind if I fart?"

"Yeah, I saw that show." A lighter flared against the filter cigarette he held in unnaturally white teeth. "So, let's talk." I sensed his preparation of himself, his decision to go on the offensive. "For starters, how come you weren't around when our Lear tried to pick you up?"

"That's what I want you to tell me."

"Me? Look, you wanted to know about *Brideshead*, you squeezed the info out of us, and we sent down the plane. And then you didn't show. I don't mind looking silly, but your disappearance kind of rattled the cages at Huntsville."

"My sudden reappearance should rattle them even more."

"What's on your mind, Steve?"

"Come on." I looked into the face of an old friend who became more recognizable by the minute; the familiar face materialized in the unfamiliar frame of time and age and new flesh. So I shoved all the death between us, hanging tough.

"You think we did something to you?"

"You bet."

"Do you mind telling me what we did?"

"You want the case against you?"

"What happens afterward? You going to use that gun?" He nodded at my pocket.

"Maybe."

"Must have a hell of a case." But his mind was working very fast now, as he assessed the dimensions of his problem.

"A hell of a case," I said. I got up and locked the den door, hearing distant rock music from upstairs as I did. "Who's home?"

"My daughter, the younger one, who let you in. Wife's out with the other. Cat's out. Dog's in back." His mind raced; he measured the distance between us.

"Don't try to jump me, Les. Don't give me an excuse, man." Surprising to learn from somewhere within that you're ready to shoot an old friend.

He subsided a little, aged, diminished into the leatherette of his swivel chair. "Tell me." His voice grew old with him; the abrasions in it had smoothed.

So I told him. "I called you two days ago. Night before last we made our deal on *Brideshead*. A few hours later somebody pumped five slugs into a lady who was sleeping where I usually sleep."

"Jesus," he said. "How do you . . .?"

"Wait. Wait. Last night I was booked on Eastern Flight seventy-three. That's the one that blew up off Jacksonville. Twenty-four people dead on that one. Twenty-five, if you include me."

"Steve, you don't think we . . ."

"Hell I don't, man. This morning I rented a plane and pilot in Miami and flew up. An F–4 tried to ram us near Charleston. The fucking *FAA* steered us in among some TV towers coming into D.C."

"You think NASA'd line up something like this?"

"To protect a little science someplace? You bet."

"We don't kill, Steve. We really don't."

"I always thought that."

"It's true." He studied me, like a psychiatrist weighing my neurosis, testing the range of my paranoia. "Let me tell you how things look from my side, okay?" I nodded. "I've been on the phone making giant-sized concessions on *Brideshead* to my old friend and colleague. I've spent agency dough getting a plane down to pick you up. I've smoothed things between you and me and the Huntsville people, so they *won't* kill you when they see you. Speak daggers but use none, okay? And everything seems cool, even kind of productive. The press will be represented after all. *Brideshead* could look goddamned heroic." He sensed my impatience at going over old ground and held up a modulating palm. "So that's how things lie. But then tonight, you show up here, a *gat* in your pocket, looking like Raskolnikov for Christ's sake, and tell me somebody *big* is trying to hit you, and hitting everybody around you in the process, and that somebody is me. Put yourself in my place, Steve. What does it sound like?"

"It sounds like the definitive page from the paranoid's handbook."

"Sure it does."

"But it isn't, Les. This thing is happening. It can't happen without some pervasive kind of control over things like air-traffic controllers. And you know it. You're a very convincing guy. That's your line of work. I'm not sure but what you're shitting me, buying time; because I know and if you're in it you know that if we sit here long enough they'll track me down to your little office and blow me away. See, I don't *have* any other big enemies."

"It isn't me. It isn't us. *If* it exists, okay? I'm not sure your enemy exists."

"There's the matter of timing. I pressure you. A few hours later all this death comes into my life. Strange coincidence? I don't think so."

"I wasn't the only one you pressured, Steve."

"What do you mean?"

"John Chester. I saw him after we talked the other night. Ran into him in the hall." Dunham frowned. "In fact he asked after you and I bitched a little about your leaning on me. He didn't seem to care much. So I told him he was next."

"Why next?"

"You said you wanted to talk to him about *Godfoot*. Sounded like you had a fucking bumper crop of dirt on us. So I told him. Gave him some heartburn, I think. Anyway, he said he'd call you. Did he?"

I nodded, remembering the Chester call. Christ, maybe the enemy lived there, after all. "That still makes NASA the big enemy, Les."

"Okay, okay." He shrugged, turned away, wretched with futility.

"You going down for the mission?"

"To Huntsville, yeah. If I survive the night. They're going to launch in the morning and pick up *Excalibur* sometime toward afternoon."

"Listen, I still look at the Huntsville Group as the Enemy. Going down there is throwing my unnatural life away, unless you're telling the truth." He gave nothing back, reflected nothing. "But maybe I have to go down there to open this thing up."

"Maybe so." Was he eager for me to walk into something? I couldn't tell.

"But if NASA's my enemy, I'm in deep shit if I go down."

"An agency doesn't behave like a dinosaur, man."

"It behaves like any selfish, threatened individual. Here's what I want. I want you to fly down to Huntsville with me, as my hostage. If it turns out I'm right then what you think or do isn't too important. If I'm wrong, I'll leave you at Huntsville and hope you understand enough of my situation not to hit me with a kidnap rap."

"If you're wrong about us, Steve, and you are, I'm not worth much as a hostage."

"That's a chance we all have to take together."

"You're asking me to share the risks you think you see. If your perceptions are right, I could be s.o.l. tomorrow just because of the company I keep."

"If it's just paranoia, Les, you don't have a thing to worry about."

He burst into laughter, a harsh haw-haw noise out of Boston. Then he said, "It's frightening to be in something so fucked up, Steve. I mean it's really frightening. If I had a choice I'd tell you to stuff it. Do I?"

"Nope."

"I better pack."

"Let me help."

I followed him upstairs and sat on the edge of the Dunham family bed while he pulled clothes out of an antique pine chest and stuffed them into a small bag as soft and glossy and yellowed as an old catcher's mitt. His daughter's music thumped at us from her room down the hall. Traffic shushed by out on the main road, muffled by the crowd of elms in back. When he was packed, Dunham hauled the bag to his bedroom door and put it down. "When do we leave?"

"Later tonight."

"Do I need to dress?"

"Little airplanes are kind of dirty. Better not."

"What a fucked-up mess."

"I find it so." Then, "We better go, Les."

"Sure." He went down the hall to his daughter's room, knocked, and cracked the door. "Honey, I'm going to Huntsville tonight instead of in the morning. Tell mama I'll call tomorrow." Then he hurried in, catching me off guard. I pursued him like a cop, but the door didn't slam in my face after all. He just knelt by his beautiful girl and gave her a long hug with his eyes closed. I guess he didn't think he'd ever see her again.

9

Dunham seemed to hold that thought, for we spent our trip mostly in silence. Now and then I'd glance at him, see his evil old face illuminated by passing lights, the heavy eyes, the wide-lipped mouth, all gone contemplative, fatalistic. The .38 lay in my lap, in my left hand, pointing generally toward his left kidney. My mind uttered this cultural note: An automatic shift lets you hold a gun on your front-seat passenger. He seemed to understand that a quick movement toward escape would make me use it, something I knew absolutely, but the knowledge still surprised me. And, in that journey of passing lights and reflections, hurrying across the hypotenuse of an only vaguely familiar metro area, I discerned great changes in Steven Borg. I'd passed from mere fretting to hating. Hating, you can kill.

And yet, I doubted Dunham was my man, doubted that *Brideshead* drove the conspiracy at all; but at the time I had no alternatives, and, moreover, I had nothing to support my doubts, as against having everything to support my suspicions. Dunham wasn't a bad choice of hostages. As though he'd monitored my thoughts, he said, "How come you didn't try your conspiracy on John Chester?"

Chester. He might have been better at that. Old John. "What does Chester do?"

Dunham shook his head, acting tired. "Who knows? Something between engineering and administration. Some liaison with the Defense Department I believe. Some folks thinks he's a spook. Every agency has one."

"You think he's a spook?"

"I don't know. I guess not. He's been in the engineering rank and file a hell of a long time."

"Okay." But my attention wandered, hearing Danilov say, Ask John Chester about *Godfoot* sometime when you want to be cynical. And, in every letter, something referring me back to Chester. Chester had made that dog-trainer signal to shut Danilov up. "What's *Godfoot*, Les?"

"Oh, man." Real fatigue. "*Brideshead* I knew about. *Godfoot* I don't. Not at all. Nothing, ever, honest."

"What about *Kiev Centre*?"

"Nothing, honest." Then, after a short silence, "Beginning to think I'm on the level?"

"Maybe." He shifted in his seat, and my hand tightened on the gun. "But you're all I've got, man. We're just going to have to do it."

"I know that."

Silence again, and the passing lights.

We swung off the freeway toward the motel a shade after eleven and were on the floor by quarter past, Dunham walking his loose-limbed Fred Astaire walk ahead of me, with the suggestion of the .38 linking us like climbers. I tried to let myself in. But the unfastened door fled the pressure of my key, floated open. The *déjà vu* must have shown, for Dunham looked concerned and whispered, "Jesus, Steve, you okay?" I couldn't reply. The evening had suddenly begun mimicking the night I found Marcia. I sniffed the air for smells of flesh and gunpowder and detected nothing. Nothing. And then I made out Pam against the window, a living person twenty feet away, and I let myself breathe again, motioned Dunham into the room.

"Steve?" She spoke so softly her voice barely carried across the room.

"Yeah, it's me," I replied, imitating her whisper, wondering why.

"Who's with you?"

"Les Dunham, the NASA guy."

"That's me, NASA Guy," said Dunham, raising the conversation to a normal sound level. "Your pal kidnapped me earlier this evening. You must be Bonnie."

"She's Pam Rudd," I told him.

But his humor had already flattened against the silence from Pam. My hackles rose. "Pam, what is it?"

She met me halfway, in the middle of the room, came into my arms crying. "Steve, they found us . . ."

Dunham moved toward the door, and I broke with her and covered him with the gun. No sweaty palms, either, no trembling barrel. Jesus, these mothers really taught a man how to live. "*Stay, Les.*"

"Sure, Steve. Sure." He lowered his head in an imitation of a beaten man and sat down on one of the beds.

"Who found us, Pam?"

"They. Whoever they are. *They.*"

"But what happened?"

"About an hour after you left. The door came open suddenly, and two guys in suits came in . . ."

"But where are they now?"

"Oh, Steve." She turned away, gasping.

"Try the can," Dunham suggested.

One of them, the black one, lay like a fallen sign for gray silk suits, his head at a funny angle, the left temple soggy and blue beneath the limp mask of his face. The other had drawn himself up against the tub, something wrong with one crooked leg, his gray face badly swollen. He watched me like a doomed animal, so that I had to turn away. The dead one stared at hairs and other shitting residues that had embedded themselves around the base of the john, like fossil bugs in amber. "What happened?"

Pam said, "They came in, muscling around, talking rape, wanting you. So when they . . . when they moved on me, I . . ." Her falter drew me back and I got hold of her again. "Oh, Steve, I'm such a tough lady. I've practiced my blackbelt stuff for years. But, you know, we never really give it to anybody . . ." Then she was crying hard, gulping for air. I held onto her, telling her it was okay, everything was okay, and slowly she calmed a little, enough to say, "I know it's okay, Steve. I know. It's just that everything's different now."

"Sure," I said, and, remembering my willingness to slay old Dunham, I echoed, "Sure," and looked at him. "What do you think about that paranoia now, Lester?"

"Looks better every second." His voice came low and worried. "But you know—it means you've got the wrong hostage."

"Maybe. We'll take good care of him, too," I said.

"Thanks a bunch."

"We need you to get into Huntsville for the mission."

"That's true," he said. "But what makes you think they're going to let you get that far?"

"We've got this far, man. We're improving. They're," and I nodded toward the bathroom, "getting worse."

"We best get back on the road," Pam said, pushing herself out of my grasp and sort of dusting herself off emotionally. The transformation impressed.

"Can you fly?"

"I can always fly."

I went back to survey the casualties. The live one watched me with hooded dark eyes, wondering when the end would come. I guessed he was about my age, early thirties, middle height, middle build; nondescript, dangerous. "Who's after us, pal?" I waved the .38 at him. He watched it steadily and then let his eyelids droop, indicating silence. "Slide me your wallet." He did and I scooped it up, turned through the false cards. "Mr. Nobody." His lips flickered on the edge of a grin, which he quickly controlled. I pondered killing him. He'd heard us talking about flying and Huntsville. I thought about the kick of the pistol and the red spot near his heart and shut my eyes for a second to get rid of it. Then I said, "Listen a minute. I think you think you're helping America chase down a number-one enemy of the people. If I were smart I'd finish you, but that's more your style than mine. Keep in mind that a real honest-to-Christ enemy of the people wouldn't have such qualms. Next time . . ." I couldn't go on. It was just baby talk. He returned my gaze as steadily as a large dog and didn't give a shit for my amnesties or threats. When I looked into his eyes I found nothing but mild laughter and great contempt, a pro's condescension toward an amateur.

"I got their guns," Pam said, coming up behind me, holding the heavy government iron in her two hands. "Three fifty-seven Magnums, hon. They like to shoot through engine blocks."

"And sleeping women." I took one of the big revolvers and passed her the .38.

We tore up some towels and bound and gagged the live one, who submitted as patiently as Houdini, knowing he'd be out of his cage minutes after we left him, knowing he'd have his colleagues in to clean the place up and get rid of the body, keeping the conspiracy one of phantoms, keeping it locked in the heads of Steve Borg, Pam Rudd, and Les Dunham.

I tied him to the flushing valve of the motel toilet and made him open his mouth for another length of towel and kind of shoved him around, getting him into position. And all the while he just looked at me, telling me he'd kill me when he got out of there; telling me that, in a way, he already had.

10

The only body at the field was the line boy's, not dead but terribly sleepy behind the counter where we turned in our car and paid for fuel; sleepy, that is, until he recognized us. Then his clear boy's eyes clouded with conspiracy, and I thought, Okay, this is the fucking end.

Pam said, "What's wrong?"

"Line boy's lost his cherry," I told her. Then seeing Dunham beginning to search the situation with his eyes a trifle wide, calculating the chances of some move, I added, "Watch Dunham." She turned to our hostage, who, reminded of the busted-up G-men at the motel, laid low. To the line boy I said, "How about coming out to the plane?"

He shook his head nervously, murmuring he had to watch the silent telephone.

"I insist," I told him like a good gangster, showing the Magnum. "Nobody's going to hurt you. We just want you along."

On the way to our tiedown I asked the boy if there'd been any visitors. The way he denied it told us there had. "Bullshit," I said into his frightened ear, "we know there were. Two guys in suits. Tell us what they did."

"Nothing." His voice floated high and frightened through the night. Even with the beacon and runway and taxiway lights, there's nothing darker than a small airport at one in the morning.

"We'll see." To Pam I said, "That fucker at the motel exuded sabotage. He looked at me as if they already had us."

"I'll probably just go on and check out the airplane, Steve." Like don't explain things I already know.

"Sorry."

"S'okay."

After she unlocked the Cardinal's doors I made the line boy lie down on his back under one of the main gear struts, where he couldn't just leap to his feet and run off into the night, and got Dunham into the back seat and strapped in. With the door closed he was like a monkey in a commodious box—and nearly that calm. Pam didn't turn anything on, just got her flashlight out and went around the nose very carefully, opening doors, looking at oil, looking at drained fuel, feeling every wire and every hose, letting the light trace from connection to connection. Once she said, "Sum bitch," under her breath and tinkered under the cowling with a screwdriver, but when I asked what it was she just shook her head. Then she buttoned up the engine and walked around the airplane, going over everything that moved, and found nothing. "I don't know," she said finally. "They switched wires on the magnetos so they'd burn themselves up after a little while. But there's no guarantee we couldn't just set the plane down somewhere. I think that was just placebo sabotage. But I can't find the real thing."

"Shit," I muttered. The line boy watched all this as neutrally as the guilt and terror radiating from his young, uncontrollable face permitted. I knelt by his head, put the Magnum's ugly barrel against one oil-stained ear, and asked, "What'd they do?"

He didn't respond, so I prodded his ear with the iron, and said, "People've been trying to kill us around the fucking clock, old sport. I'm tired out. Start talking or by God I'll blow off the back of your head."

But his greater fear of government men in silk suits, and a sense I wouldn't shoot him after all, and eternal hope kept him quiet. He merely trembled with his eyes shut and his head as slick with perspiration as an overheated bird's.

Pam came over. "No dice?"

I shook my head.

Then, speaking from the cabin like an offstage ghost, Dunham growled, "Just invite the little bastard to fly with us, for Christ's sake."

"You heard the man. Get in back with him."

The line boy slowly unwound from the landing gear and stood up. Dunham's suggestion had got him by the scrotum; where he'd been scared before he now was terrified. "Get in, boy, we'll all go together."

This stripped him of his greater fears and all hope. "They . . . they did something back in the tail. I don't know what . . ."

You wouldn't have seen the wire in daylight, and Pam hadn't seen it the first time around. But now it gleamed like a silver bullet, a thin wire threaded through an eyebolt on the pivoting linkage to the plane's horizontal stabilizer. Move the stabilizer much and you pulled the wire, which ran a few inches up the widening wedge of the tail cone to an eyelet on a short metal arm screwed into a four-inch-long plastic cylinder. The cylinder had been lashed in place with ducting tape. "Sum bitch," Pam whispered.

"It looks like a modified grenade," I said.

"Yeah, those guys're deadly," she replied. "But they don't fly?"

"Why's that?"

"Well, losing your tail in an airplane means you just fall to the ground, so it's a good plan. But the only time I'd move the controls far enough to pull that pin would be on my pretakeoff check. So we'd have just blown off the tail right here in Gaithersburg, or maybe on the takeoff roll. Hundred percent survival."

"You *know* they wanted us over the mountains when it blew."

"Sure they did."

"Know what this means?"

"What?"

"They're not infallible."

While we talked, we forgot our prisoners. But the line boy moved in alongside us, drawn by the magnetism of strange happenings; Dunham had got out of the Cardinal too and instead of disappearing into the darkness—he could have made it, too, and he knew it—came back and looked at the grenade. Then our eyes met and we both grinned broadly, and I squeezed his shoulder. "Guess you're not much of a hostage after all."

He laughed. "One of the worst."

"You don't have to go."

But he knew, and we knew, that the three of us were bound

now. So he said, "I still think I'll ride along. You seem to need an idea man."

"You're right."

"Ready for an idea?"

"Sure."

"Let's use that grenade out over the mountains some place."

"Good."

He used a pocketknife to sever the wire to the pin and then set about maneuvering the grenade out of its niche, a problem with the topology of a Chinese puzzle.

"What about me?" the boy wanted to know, edging away from his newfound comrades. "I still going?"

"Nope, we leave you here, man." Pam got a roll of adhesive tape out of the first-aid box. I stopped his retreat with a wave of the Magnum and moved in on him. I had him sit down on the tire of a nearby high-winged plane and taped his wrists together around the strut and his ankles together around the landing gear, so that he could almost stand, leaning on the strut.

"You can't leave me like this. I'll die."

"No such luck. Somebody'll be out and cut you loose."

So I left him. Pam had started the Cardinal and was taxiing. I circled gingerly, afraid of walking into the shining disc of the prop, and sprang into the right-hand seat. Dunham had settled into the back once more, and held his grenade like an apple in one hand, the fingers rolling it slowly. "You really strung the poor bastard up," he said, looking at the uncomfortable line boy as we taxied past.

"He wasn't too happy about it."

"What'd he say?" Pam asked.

"He said, 'For the love of God, Montresor.'"

Dunham chuckled. "This work's hardening your heart."

"So it is," I said.

"And our brains, too," Pam put in. "Who guaranteed us the grenade was all they did to the plane?"

11

But it was. We climbed out through the darkness, the city a rolling field of light abruptly split by the dark paths of rivers slicing through. The altimeter unwound until we were near five thousand feet; the transponder signaled everyone where we were. If *they* were watching the radar and saw a plane leave Gaithersburg, they might monitor it for the explosion. She carried all the running lights and strobes, too, in case someone watched.

As we passed Front Royal, crossed the first ridge of the Appalachians, she slowed the Cardinal and I cracked the passenger door. Then Dunham, grinning like a boy, closed the lever on the grenade and dropped it into the night. As he did, Pam cut the power, shut off our lights and transponder, and let us glide in near silence into the valley. Behind and below us a bright flame opened the night for an instant and was swallowed in darkness.

The ridges rose on either side of us, darker than the night sky. She kept us low and unlighted, flying the time-rounded folds of these old mountains southward, westward, following the meager lights on the two-lanes and interstates a few hundred feet below. "Nobody," she said at one point, "builds towers in the middle of a highway."

She didn't mention power lines strung across valleys. The first one approached us with only the airplane warning balls visible, like alien spaceships. Then the cable and balls whipped by overhead, causing me to shake my head with wonder and spend less time looking forward.

Dunham dozed in the back seat. I admired his clear conscience, and wondered how clear it really was. Having been absolved and pardoned from the trip, why had he come along? Or, going a step further, what if he weren't involved in the conspiracy, but the *Brideshead* people were? That meant he and Pam and I would be walking into the same shit storm in Huntsville. And what if Dunham and *Brideshead* and all of that were just blind turns? Then where did I look for the BFE?

To Chester, perhaps. To spooks in every agency. To the teeming life under the great rock of government. A little light might get them off our backs. I kept believing that.

I looked over at Pam. Fatigue had begun to work on her features, drawing everything down; her eyes were heavy, and she kept opening the air vent for a little rush of cool air, a shot of oxygen. "Wish I knew how to fly," I told her.

"Me too, hon. But it's not very far, don't fret."

"A man'd be crazy to worry about you."

"Don't know that I like being somebody you wouldn't worry about."

"Okay, I'm worried."

"Better."

"I'm worried about your not answering the phone when we get back to Miami."

"Think we'll get back?"

"Yeah, I do." Then after reflecting, "I'm pretty sure we will."

"Think you'll call?"

"Don't you?"

"I don't know." She winked and returned to her flying, left me sorry for us and less certain about our prospects than I had been. So I put my hand on the high, tough curve of her thigh, causing her to shudder and to smile for me.

Off to the southeast, the sky cleared to gray, and then went a little golden, coloring us where we flew below the level of the still-shadowed ridges. With daylight coming, Pam climbed the Cardinal back up to three thousand feet, getting less conspicuous than a highway-hugging airplane. From there the undulating north-south folds of rock and soil and trees ran out beneath the dawn, the valleys here and there cupping ponds of fog, silvered by the approaching sun that still hid below the horizon. And then, looking to the northwest, where the sky hung in dark, indigo folds, I saw a beautiful sight: One of the visible stars was moving toward us, a reddish gold star, gleaming steadily brighter and brighter, moving fast acoss the dark dome of sky, "Pam, look," I said, and pointed at the object. "It's *Excalibur*."

We watched the metal star cross overhead and disappear into the dawn to the southeast, and both of us were awed and touched by the event. It seemed an omen to me, and I think to her as well, but whether for good fortune or ill winds we couldn't say. And when it was gone we looked at one another, shook our heads in appreciation of the event, and turned away into our separate silences.

The Tennessee River ran south off to our left, spreading like a minor sea behind its chain of dams, shedding its fog beneath the sun, which now bulged over the eastern rim of Earth. The big river snaked southward to a city Pam said was Chattanooga, where everything converged.

She turned the plane west, followed the river a few minutes more, and then left it as it curled to the south. Huntsville lay off in the haze ahead of us, a middling town made smaller and flattened by distance into vague grids and plumes of smoke where the hills ended and the shallow eastern slope of the Mississippi Valley began. Beyond Huntsville, Wheeler Lake shone like another sea, a hundred-mile-long monument to the damming propensities of the Corps of Engineers. "The beautiful and the dammed," I told Pam's ear. She laughed.

Gradually the town congealed into pale buildings on a grid among trees and rivers, pretty except for the tentacles of big highways flowing into it. South of the town against the river lay the low buildings of Redstone Arsenal and NASA's Marshall Research Center. Pam banked us past them and to the south, steering along the river. "I'm putting in a few miles down the road," she said. "They'll be watching for us in Huntsville."

"They."

She echoed, "They."

I turned to wake Dunham, who stirred beneath the early morning sun, popped his old, knowing eyes open suddenly, like a dog waking up, and quickly got his bearings.

"Huntsville off to starboard," I said.

"Shonuff." He took it in, watched the NASA buildings slide by beneath the right-hand wing. "That's the place. Where're we landing?" He leaned forward so Pam could hear him over the engine.

"Pryor, up the road a piece," she said.

"Oh," he grunted and relaxed into his seat. I looked at him closely, trying to squeeze out an insight or two that would keep me a jump ahead. But he'd gone opaque—or perhaps *was* as innocent as a wrinkled old baby—for he radiated nothing I could use.

Pam took us west along the river. To the north the arsenal stretched out like a sparsely settled city. Huntsville airport went by on our right, the runways almost calling to us. Then she pulled back on the power a little and we coasted down a shallow dive, and in a minute she was on the radio with her fake airplane number telling traffic at the Pryor airport where she was and what she planned to do. The wheels poked out of the Cardinal, she added flaps, and came around to the south to land, the narrow mile of runway pointing off toward Wheeler Lake and the low-lying, sun-lit city of Decatur across the water.

We were able to rent a four-year-old blue Chevy at Pryor, a car whose primer had begun to peek through everywhere and whose interior smelled like large men who worked hard. I drove, Pam had the right-hand seat for a change, and Dunham rode in back, navigating. Life had become more relaxed since we'd stopped pointing guns at one another.

At the Arsenal, a black MP who looked about fourteen waved us aside to a visitor's center, where we dismounted and signed in, Dunham pushing with his NASA ID while Pam and I decided in a short aside that we better use our real names. We reasoned that if the *Brideshead* people were the BFE it didn't matter what names we used, since we were now in their camp. So we signed in and shuffled around the brown-and-black linoleum and looked at the green walls and their various bulletins and admonitions, while the WAC behind the information counter ate her fingernails and talked to somebody on the phone. After a while we sat down on the leatherette office sofas lining one wall and waited, Dunham said, for one of the *Brideshead* group to come get us. "They're down in the shuttle area, which is restricted. So we have to be escorted in."

It took about twenty minutes for our escort to arrive, a small-ish slender man whose olive suit and aura pushed him into the background. His skin was slick, ivory, thinly filled with the blood of some petered out line that had been old at the beginning of European time; he wore the unhappy smile of the immigrant aris-tocrat, frail with cultural displacement. So I didn't notice him when he first came in and wouldn't have, except Dunham leaped up and said, "Dr. Wellman, I'm Les Dunham, NASA–Washington." He shook hands with the little man, who did not quite click his heels, and then introduced us. Working from a ducal reflex, Wellman emitted maximum charm at Pam, in the expecta-tion she would fall at his feet. But he could just barely control his disappointment in me, keeping his oversized face a few degrees averted, saying, "I am glad to meet you, Mr. Borg," and giving me a cold, little hand to grasp.

"Me too," I said.

He shrugged. "Come, Mr. Dunham. You can follow in your car."

We filed out after him and trailed his blue NASA sedan off into the Arsenal grounds. Redstone is one of those immense military reservations where you can drive an hour and see nothing much beyond some street signs and sharecropping cotton patches and cattle munching the scorched summer grass in open fields. NASA's big administration building, white and configured like a stern-wheeler, drifted by, and still we pushed out through the Arsenal lands. The big engine test-stands rose like middling sky-scrapers from the scrub and pine, and bunkers seemed to be everywhere, as though there weren't an acre where some kind of ordnance hadn't been tested or stored.

"Velcome to Pennemunde," I said.

"Don't be a shit," Dunham responded from the back seat.

"He's just a little old man, now," Pam said.

"And besides," Dunham put in, "when they came over they gave us all they had, everything. We owe them for it."

"Sure we do. Ever meet a scientist who wouldn't do his thing if somebody'd fund it?"

"Who's Wellman?" Pam wanted to know.

"A German," I said.

"Come on," Dunham said. "He was captured by U.S. forces at Pennemunde. Came over to Texas, then to Huntsville, with Von Braun and company. Boy, talk about culture shock. Anyway, he's one of the few Germans left here."

"Does he have a specialty?" I asked.

"Let's see. I think he designed the solar experiments on the early shuttle flights."

"Just what we need," I said. "Another solar astronomer."

Wellman led us deep into the Arsenal, so deep we began to drift into nervousness, exchanging loaded looks, going quiet. But then we took another turn off through the piney woods that brought us to a gate with an army guard on it. Wellman took a minute with him; we saw the young man nod with comprehension, and then he waved us through after the blue sedan.

"We're in the shuttle test area now," Dunham said, speaking in a low voice, as though we'd entered the nave of his church.

A huge test-stand rose nearby, the scale not quite believable, like the assembly buildings at Kennedy, and we began to see more of the low, white cinderblock structures that clustered here and there in the Arsenal. The narrow-gauge railroads used to move heavy ordnance ran between them, antique and rusted in the tall grass. Wellman turned into a reserved parking space near one of the buildings, and we parked next to him. He met us on the asphalt, deferential to Pam, cold to me. "Now," he told Dunham, "you vill come vith me."

Not much of the antique Arsenal flavor survived inside the place, which had been gutted to serve NASA, with a row of small, light offices for the scientists, some benchwork labs for the technicians, and, filling one end of the structure, a shuttle control room that replicated part of the manned spaceflight facility in Houston, but in miniature. Tense faces looked up from video screens as we entered but then returned to the parade of numbers flashing there. The crew was small, half a dozen people I took to be mostly senior scientists. Wellman took us to a conference room behind the control area and asked us to sit down to meet what Dunham had called the Huntsville Group.

12

"Let me introduce you," Wellman began, delicately stopping between us and the four people who'd entered the room behind us.

"Never mind, Helmut," a thin, white-haired Englishman said from the far side. "We'll just go around. I know Les. I assume you're Mr. Borg, and. . . ?"

"Pam Rudd," she said, nodding.

"She's my pilot," I added.

"Quite a retinue for a reporter," he said. "But, anyway, I'm Brendan James, and I suppose you'd call me the putative leader of the Huntsville Group. Sounds like a band of captured freedom marchers. But we've only got these two minorities, Dr. David Yamaha," and he indicated a Japanese of indeterminate youth, who nodded, "an aerospace engineer with a distinguished industrial surname; and Danielle Moreau," indicating a bronze-haired blond in her fifties, once beautiful, now merely awesome, "who is in biosystems. Dr. Richard Eiger is our other Kraut," and he waved at a slender blond-haired young man of about thirty, who nodded coldly. "And of course there are a few others who couldn't leave their stations. You can meet them later. We have a few more of our subversive little group scattered through the agency. Les is one, for we always wondered if we wouldn't have to announce something after we finished *Brideshead*. There are others down at the Cape, in Houston, in headquarters . . ."

"Like John Chester?" I probed.

"No, not like John Chester." He paused, trying to arrest unfriendly feelings. Then, "We didn't think John was right for *Brideshead*. No reflection. Just not quite right."

"Other loyalties?"

"You might say that. But, to continue. There are just the half dozen of us you see here and in the control room. The reason we're into *Brideshead* at all is that we contributed to the original mistake. Now you could say we're paying for our sins by massively misappropriating government funds." Polite laughter. "When the early shuttle was up and working, we had this backup control center here, which turned out to be too redundant and was never used. But it was a perfect arrangement for *Brideshead*. Once our bird was up, we wanted to control her from here and leave the Houston and Kennedy people clear of our little subterfuge. I think that's all you need to know right now. The bird is up and chasing *Excalibur*. We should pull up on it soon. NORAD's latest reentry forecast puts it at about eighteen Zulu tomorrow, which will be two tomorrow afternoon here. Now I suggest you find seats in our hall and watch the proceedings. When it's over, Mr. Borg, we'll be happy to answer any questions. After all, you're the whole press corps for this one."

It wasn't the kind of talk the BFE would give once you came within his grasp. I saw Dunham studying me and said, "Tell them my sad story. I've got to get my camera." Wellman guided me out to the car, where I retrieved the Nikon and a clean notebook, and brought me back. The group in the conference room were in mild shock at what they'd heard from Dunham.

"Helmut," James said, "Les tells us someone's been trying to murder Mr. Borg since he got onto *Brideshead*. There's been a lot of killing already, big-government-style stuff I gather. He thought it was us."

The German smiled sweetly. "It vasn't, of course." Then, "I mean, ve vould have loved to have had you fade away, Mr. Borg. Ve didn't need the press in here for this. But ve couldn't think of how to make you fade away."

There came a murmur of agreement from the others, to which I nodded, saying, "That's reassuring. But if you're not . . ."

And James interrupted, picking up my unstated idea, "Who is? Your enemy must be someone else."

"And you've led him to us," Wellman said.

"Maybe I have," I said.

"Jesus," moaned Dunham, "we didn't think this one through, did we?"

"Although," Wellman put it now, "perhaps there is no connection betveen vhat they vant and *Brideshead. You* may be hunted, but *ve* may not be involved."

"Thanks."

"Besides," James said, "we're in a restricted area. If they want you or us, they have to wait till we come out."

"They've been able to use air-traffic control to get us. I don't see them faltering over the murder of one army guard."

"Only if they vant us too," Wellman said. "But I begin to think ve are not involved."

I didn't know how to argue the other side, but I believed in it still. Somewhere in all this, another facet of government stalked us southward to Huntsville, had perhaps used us to locate *Brideshead.* Perhaps they closed the net as we pondered. The impulse to run flowed through me, strong as grief; but then I forced it down and said, "Okay."

And while I loosened my grip on those realities, a messenger arrived from the control room to give us, play fashion, a glimpse of more. "Dr. James," he said, "we're coming up on the last orbit now, visual contact in one zero."

James and his colleagues forgot me, forgot us, very quickly. They hurried out into the twilight of the control room, and we followed with Wellman, who put us in three airline-type seats near the back wall, facing a screen big enough to carry a heavyweight championship fight, but blank at the moment. I felt—the three of us felt, I think—how absolutely we were the strangers in the room. A face would look up, illuminated by the cathode-ray tube display, study us, watch us, puzzle over us, then go back to the technical world that was stable. It made me feel strange, anomalous, like a traveler in time.

"Very well," James said on the loudspeaker, "we have it." Other voices murmured in the room and occasionally one would utter a time reference: "*Brideshead* in eight."

Suddenly the screen lit up with a jumpy set of raster lines, then gradually resolved itself into a color television view from the *Brideshead* vehicle. "We've got video," James said. "Visual contact in three." The lower part of the screen showed the slow-wheeling lines and whorls of clouds, the indigo rim of the atmosphere breaking the picture about in half horizontally, and dark space filling the upper half. My skin puckered with goosebumps, seeing my world from this robot eye two hundred miles high. Pam shared the sensation and squeezed my hand. And I thought of the degree of luck that put me here, where history was going to be rough-drafted, maybe made, while every other reporter in the country moved in on Houston, the Cape, JPL, anywhere they thought they could cover a story they couldn't see; and the networks no doubt had their planes ready to launch, reasoning that if they could just bring it off the world would be able to see it after all.

We didn't perceive *Excalibur* immediately when it rose from the horizon ahead of the faster *Brideshead* vehicle. Then a white flash against the curve of Earth showed us where the derelict flew. "We have visual contact," James said. *Brideshead,* flying a slightly larger orbit, moved inexorably in on the larger ship. I marveled internally. Everything was being directed by a computer, playing the masses and velocities of the two craft against the invisible strings of gravity that tied the orbits to a common point near the center of the planet.

The flash told us where to look. Now, as we watched, it evolved into the familiar form of the shuttle, a gleaming airplane of space flying away from us. Its cargo doors were folded open, and we could make out the dome of what looked like a solar experiment; a reddish shell-shaped object extended parallel to the vertical stabilizer on a long telescoping boom.

"Okay," I said, turning to Dunham, "*now* tell me what the payload is."·

His eyes narrowed and he thought about what he was seeing, trying, I thought, to place the objects in the cargo bay. Finally he said, "Steve, I wasn't shitting you. I really didn't know what the bird had aboard. Nobody did except the Air Force, okay?" I nodded and he went on. "But I'm a pretty avid reader of *Aviation Week*. That turret just aft of the docking adapter, the dome with all the telescopes sticking out, looks like a laser-weapon installation

I've seen pictures of. They had something like it on a KC–135 airborne laser laboratory out at Kirtland. Well, you have a big laser, you need power, rots and rots of power. So I guess that thing sticking up by the tail is a variant of the old SPAR reactor; it was only a matter of time before we had to put nuclear power on the shuttle. It's probably designed to come apart on reentry. But, you know, the way the ship is oriented, I bet it shields the reactor from much reentry heating so it'll come back in as well. So . . . it's a dirty sort of bomb, Steve. A dirty sort of bomb."

Now we could see the yawing movement of the spaceship, one end sweeping slowly back and forth like a caudal fin through the plane of its orbit, majestic and gentle, like the swinging of all ponderous, well-hinged objects, all large masses unconstrained by gravity.

"Dr. James, Houston for you on line four," one of the aides said over the intercom. I watched James break from the group of controllers and pick up the phone. He frowned as he took the message, asked some questions, and put the phone down with something like resignation. When he'd finished he strolled over to Wellman, avoiding my eyes, and said, "I need to talk to you, Helmut."

"Me too, Dr. James," I intruded. "No point in excluding the press now."

"Or anyone else," he admitted wearily. "I imagine you've been scooped, Mr. Borg. Houston says NORAD's moved up their prediction. They have *Excalibur* reentering in seven more revolutions. NASA's announced it. State's requested Russian help."

"Why Russian?"

"They want them to use a killer satellite to shoot it down."

"But why would they?" *The people ready their rockets. . . .*

"Because the footprint centers on Kiev."

"Jesus," I said and thought, Yeah, *really* classified.

"*Godfoot,*" said Wellman.

The word pushed me into silence, as the situation did the others. For a moment everything was immobilized by the advancing *Brideshead* vehicle on the screen. Then Wellman broke it with, "Vell, ve can see the ship. Ve can see it has more than any seven revolutions before it comes in."

James nodded. "That means they can bring her in on command. Bring her in on Kiev, if they want."

I said, "What's *Godfoot?*"

"Sometime maybe I tell you, Mr. Borg," Wellman replied. "If ve succeed and push the hulk into the sea, maybe I tell you. And maybe not." He paused and then added, "You should ask your friend, John Chester."

"Or Vladimir Danilov?"

"I begin to see vhy you have a problem, Mr. Borg." He turned away, talking again to James. "Ve have an opportunity here, Brendan. Ve can continue with *Brideshead* and keep the reentry clear of the Soviet Union."

"I think we have to do that," James said.

Their technical problems drew them away from me, and they rejoined the group controlling the mission, where a quick huddle was held over strategy before they got back into their stations. I got out the Nikon and began blasting away with high-speed film, hoping to get silhouettes, lights, and the view from our flying robot.

As we watched, the flying camera passed above the derelict; then, minutes later, slowed, fell like an electron into the lower orbit. Murmured commands and the robot eye swung around one hundred eighty degrees, picking up *Excalibur* behind it now, yawing ponderously, like a swimming whale.

James said on the loudspeaker, "The word is that *Excalibur* is coming down on Kiev in another seven revolutions. It carries an armed high-energy laser and a one-megawatt reactor that appears to be out of control. So the Russians may try to shoot it down with one of their killer satellites. It sounds full of intrigue to me, and I'm not certain they have the capability. In the meantime, I think we must proceed. We have only a little time, but perhaps we can get some science out of this as well. We'll take *Brideshead* back along the fuselage and try to make out what happened up there. Then we'll hook on the nose as best we can and retrofire the whole package in such a way that the reactor is destroyed by reentry."

There followed a burst of agitated movement around the consoles as people rested their fannies, quickly stretched, settled further into their seats. Then everyone got serious again, while the three of us watched like children in a dream.

The *Brideshead* vehicle canted slightly and, like a whaleboat steering gingerly along the flank of a living whale, floated back along *Excalibur*'s left side. Not even superficial dings showed in the pale skin. I thought: It's so fucking lonely out there that even meteors are rare. For no reason at all, watching the robot eye run over the big derelict, I thought of the horror of being left up there, endlessly orbiting, or, rather, orbiting until gravity won the struggle . . .

. . . whether we see ghosts in space, or the string of gravity that holds us up or pulls us down . . .

Danilov's voice haunting me while I peered through a camera at his cold, lonesome province.

"NORAD say's Russia's launched a killer satellite from Tyuratam, contact in thirty-seven minutes," Moreau said on the loudspeaker.

"Not to worry," James responded, also on the loudspeaker.

Our robot eye still moved along the metal skin of *Excalibur*, rotating up and down to inspect the structure and external gear. Then they reversed the drift, thrusting *Brideshead* forward until it rode once more ahead of the larger ship and in line with it. "Okay," James said on the speaker, "we'll move in and try to clamp on the nose. Keep the camera going, we'd like a look inside. See if the radiation's produced any giant bacteria or anything." But there was no laughter: All of us knew we'd see death up there, and tensed for it.

The probe floated in toward the more or less cheerful, black-and-white whale face of *Excalibur*, the windscreens like dark, downturned eyes. "Let's zoom in for an interior shot before we dock," James said. The camera seemed to enter the flight deck, the shifting patterns of sharp darks and lights, like the below-decks sunlight in a gently rolling ship. At first, the shapes in the foreground appeared to be some kind of gear restrained against the buoyancy of zero gravity. But then, as light swept them, we saw

123 |

the remains of the two exploded men strapped there, their faces limp, torn masks upon their skulls, the cabin full of the drifting globular fluids that their internal pressure had squeezed out of them.

Pam said, "Oh, Lordy."

"God," said Dunham.

"Terrible thing," James said on the loudspeaker. "A bloody terrible terrible thing." And then, almost musing, he said, "Well, it looks like a pressure-vessel failure. Probably that damnable laser back there, pumped up and pumped up and then something pops and a bloody fireball cracks the pressure hull. God."

That was all the scientists said about what had happened that left *Excalibur* dead in orbit, dead and filled with dead. But my mind could not leave them. I drifted there, remembering empathetically the sudden rash of nameless trouble and budding fear that ended when the fireball let the vacuum of space in upon them, gave them time barely to utter "Houston" before their blood began to boil, their bodies to explode. And so they suspended like dead men in a sunken ship, buoyant, destroyed by differences in pressure, and yet to some degree preserved by the great inhospitality that had killed them.

But the horror had just begun.

At first, a floating shape in the background seemed to be loose packing; but then, as the shifting light touched the bulky object we saw it was a spacesuit, another body. When the derelict yawed, a bulkhead would slap the body softly, send it tumbling across the small, grim compartment to the far wall, which sent it tumbling back on the return. The figure was shunted forward this way, surfacing closer and closer to our camera, until it bumped the windshield. And there, for a long, horrible second, our screen filled with this face frozen in the terrified sleep of suffocation, a cry somewhere behind the swollen boy lips, somewhere in the dead brain behind the fair, pudgy face. "Jesus Christ," I prayed. "It's Danilov."

Pam didn't understand the reference, but Dunham did. "What the hell's . . .?"

But I was remembering:

The great star trembles,
Ready to fall,
The Godfoot,
Stepping on Kiev.
The people watch from their shadows,
Readying rockets for
Cosmonaut sappers
To keep the star from
Kiev Centre.

I thought I knew it all.

13

The whole room suspended, everyone hypnotized by Danilov's drifting body. For a time some dynamic fluke in the motion of *Excalibur* returned him again and again, pressed the helmeted face toward the camera, filling our screen. Then, slowly, the motion of the giant spacecraft swept him away from us, bumped him down toward the far end of the flight deck. I lowered the Nikon, watched him float into the shadows, out of sight.

Brendan James came over. "What do you make of that?"

Reluctant to share what I thought I knew—and uncertain of my knowledge—I just shook my head.

The loudspeaker said, "NORAD puts the Russian bird in *Excalibur's* orbit, estimates intercept in ten."

James said, "I mean, why put him up there at all?"

Wellman answered. "They have their plots too, Brendan. Ve tell them *Excalibur* vill reenter over Kiev, ve arrange even to make it happen, to force a demonstration of their killer satellite. They counterplot and put Cosmonaut Danilov into *Excalibur*, possibly vith explosives they can detonate from the ground. This guarantees their satellite's performance."

"But it isn't just the dead cosmonaut," James said. "Look at the instrument panels. They're all lit up."

I looked and saw what he'd seen: *Excalibur* lived if its crew did not; so NASA could have brought the ship home under computer control—or, at worst, steered it into the sea. "Who told the big lie, Les? You?"

"Come on," he bristled. "I keep telling you and you keep not listening. Listen to me. This one wasn't under our control, beyond some housekeeping help. It was a military launch. They monitored the activities aboard. We got to participate on the PR side. You know, television broadcasts of the launch, smiling astronauts, and that's about all. So when we heard from the Air Force that the ship was dead, we assumed the ship was dead. I mean," and he gave a sour smirk, "would they lie? To *us?*"

"You know what this means?" James put in. "It means this man Danilov could have radioed his plight to the world and perhaps forced us to bring him back in. But he didn't. Why?"

Wellman responded. "He vas a kind of patriot finally. He believed so much ve should not have this dirty sort of thing in space that he vould not expose it, even to save himself."

We all nodded wisely.

"Killer satellite intercepting in three," the loudspeaker said.

James had been musing. "You know, if we bring her down, our country loses some crucial intelligence."

"Not at all," Wellman argued. "Ve don't *know* there are explosives aboard. If they bring her down, ve only know they brought her down. Maybe ve overestimate their level of skill. Maybe not. But I tell you, Brendan, space is novhere to have this kind of foul *merde* happening. It truly is not."

"Let's do this," James said, his eyes almost closed with decision making. "Let's turn *Brideshead* about for a look at the Soviet bird, then proceed."

"That vould be good," Wellman nodded.

James returned to his command console. "Service-engine retrofire in three," he said. "But in the meantime, let's rotate our bird around to look at the Russian."

As we watched, our camera eye swung away from *Excalibur*, from the astronauts' tomb, and irised out to infinity. And there, just a gleaming point, we saw the approaching killer spacecraft, drifting it seemed slowly but clearly overtaking the derelict. The camera stayed with it and zoomed in for a closeup, showing us the twin spheres, the cylindrical warhead, the antennae; a silent, ominous insect, pale bodied and marked with a red star. I felt I was looking into the hollow eyeholes of World War III. "Okay," James ordered, "let's do our thing."

Our camera rotated back to the derelict. "We're moving in to connect now." Then, as the video picture shivered with the impact, "We have contact. We are docked."

"Verify position."

"Computer verifies reentry over one seven three east, four south, descending node. Footprint centered southeast of Pitcairn."

"Oxidizer chamber pressure coming up."

"Propellant chamber pressure coming up."

"Program for five-minute burn."

"Helium pressure up in both tanks."

"Fire in one."

The murmured litany rolled over us, hypnotic, reassuring.

". . . nine, eight, seven . . ."

"HOLD IT!" someone yelled from the door.

Four men stood behind us. I recognized the cat from Gaithersburg first, and he recognized me with narrowed eyes and a cold smile that said maybe he'd have his chance today. It took me longer to identify John Chester as the speaker—not because he'd changed, but because he hadn't. The years since Apollo–Soyuz had not touched his face or altered his haircut or dress, as all the years before had not. He stepped out of the 1950s, the crew cut, narrow-tied, white-shirted engineer, his thin mouth held in a neutral, thoughtful purse. Light flashed off his little wire-rimmed mad-scientist glasses as he looked around the room. "Hold it," he repeated without yelling, using the voice I remembered, a homosexual bray; but it came on so calm, with such authority, I thought for a moment he'd have his way with us.

"Hello, John," James said. "What's all the excitement?"

"I should ask you, Brendan. I mean, this is quite a little secret you've kept from the agency."

"My agency or yours, John?"

"Funny."

"Rather."

"Too bad it isn't going anywhere. *Excalibur* comes down on Kiev, unless the killer satellite can stop it. Period. We let things run their course." He scanned the room, stopping at Wellman. "Helmut, nice to see you. Dr. Wellman," he continued, "is the only one here who knows why it has to come down on Kiev." Chester kept scanning until he came to me. "He and maybe Steven Borg of the Miami *Herald*. Not much press for this mission, Steve. The lady must be your pilot. How do *you* do? And I know Les. Hi, Les."

"Hello, John," Dunham muttered. The quartet had him as nervous as the rest of us, and he couldn't keep from staring, like a deer looking into the lights of an approaching car.

"We all know why you want it, John," I said. "But it doesn't do you any good. There's a cosmonaut on *Excalibur*. Danilov. We saw him."

"Really? How interesting." He didn't believe me.

"You know what it means?"

"It doesn't mean diddly to me, Steve. Jack Kennedy could be alive on *Excalibur* and it would still go in on Kiev, and they'd still have to try their satellite on it. Priorities."

"It means the satellite demonstration's rigged."

"We still want the demonstration. We put a lot into it. Now we're going to get it."

"Well, you're welcome to it, I suppose," James said, feinting away from his console so that his body hid what his right hand was doing. On the television screen the picture vibrated wildly as the rockets came up. Chester emitted an involuntary yell, which made one of his assistants haul out one of those big government pistols, but Chester made him put it back. James ignored them, kept his weight on the switch that ordered the Apollo module's engine to mix the explosive torrent of nitrogen tetroxide and hydrazine. "We have ignition," he said in the voice Sidney Carton used on the scaffold.

We watched the screen, saw the vibration increase as the engines on *Brideshead* came up to a full burn, and then everything steadied as *Excalibur* slowed and began to fall toward the denser atmosphere. "We're going down," James said on the intercom, "one five zero nautical miles now, and going down . . ."

A bright flash illuminated part of the screen, the exploding of some distant star. "The killer satellite just detonated," James said. "We're well out of range."

"And there vere no explosives on *Excalibur*," Wellman murmured loud enough that I could hear him.

"Danilov decided not to play," I told him. Vlad had carried his sapper's burden to the satellite, planted his charge, and then, in the hour or day or week he lived on *Excalibur*, disarmed it.

Wellman and I looked at one another a long time before the loudspeaker drew us back to *Brideshead*. "One two zero nautical miles . . . one hundred . . . we've got reentry now, seventy miles and we've got reentry . . ."

Brideshead was the first object to rip away from *Excalibur*, as the collision with the atmosphere tore at the big ship. Our view spun wildly, and James came on the intercom, saying, "Steady the camera, get the camera back on *Excalibur*, steady . . ." In a moment we had a shaky look at the reentering shuttle, the fuselage bright with heat, with now and then the spark of a shattered tile hurled into a slipstream made of glowing lights. A crimson cloud flowed across the cargo bay as the laser dome ripped away and discharged its huge energies. The reactor whipped on its boom, threatening to tear away even as it began to incandesce, and then exploded in a shower of sparks, a little more radioactivity for the planet's magnetic field, to circle, returning slowly, slowly . . . But now the camera showed us only its own fiery end. The screen went black.

From there, our minds had to follow *Excalibur* down—the great glider, silent, white hot, diving back through the high upper atmosphere with its following cloud of sparkling debris, which one would see from a ship below as a sudden gathering of stars, great ones and minuscule ones, that winked on, shot across the sky, and winked out; the shuttle and its pieces, all cooling on their long fall toward the southern ocean; and finally their splashing in, utterly shattered, *Excalibur* sinking with her cargo of dead men, taking them to sleep with all the other buried men amid the ancient muds and bones and fish turds, lost ships, and bottom dwellers in the seafloor two miles deep.

"You've really fucked things up, Brendan," Chester said into the preoccupied silence that followed. "You've really fucked things up good."

"My next bumper sticker," James said, "will be something like No Spooks in Space."

"You'll have plenty of time to work it out," Chester said. "The amount of misappropriated money is substantial. I doubt you'll even be given bail. I doubt anyone will see you again for a long time." As the people in the room began to move around, Chester's bully boys got out their iron, making everyone go quiet again.

I said, "We're just bystanders, John. You can't hold me, or Pam, or even Les Dunham."

"I know that, Steve. I know that. You can go. So can your pilot, and Les. You can even take Dr. Wellman, to steer you out. I can find him if I need him."

We looked at one another, stupefied, and began to pick up our things. Maybe, I thought, maybe this is it. They got their misappropriators of funds, now they forget about us. Doesn't exactly make full sense, but it makes some. Maybe that's how the government operates. To Brendan James we could only give a long look and a shake of the head. But he said, "Don't worry, Mr. Borg. It was our show. We knew it wasn't free."

So Wellman led us out past Chester and his GS–13 hit men to our car, got into ours with us, and off we went, past the innocent young guard at the gate, back into the wildnerness of the Arsenal, letting survival call the tune, driving off, unskeptical . . . But then Dunham cocked his monkey head, listened a moment, and growled, *"Fuck!"*

I listened hard and finally heard the beating of a chopper. A few seconds later it flattened around a turn behind us, not quite below the trees, a Huey Cobra trailing us head down, like a hungry mantis, overtaking us quickly. Soon it would bring those guns or maybe its rockets to bear and we'd be eternally s.o.l. I tried a few sharp, car-ruining turns, but the ship just drifted after us, four times as fast, ten times more maneuverable. As we sped past the built-up area around the NASA administration building, it broke off, indicating that Chester's side didn't want too much visibility; but then, as we found ourselves once more in a tunnel of pines and live oaks, the chopper returned, getting up close, where there wouldn't be any question of survivors. It fired a burst from its cannons, and we felt a couple of the rounds slam into the trunk and explode. The rear window showered us with glass. Wellman said, "*Gott!*" and fell forward. Pam got over the seat back quickly, pushed him against the door, and tore his coat to press the cloth into the mess where his left shoulder had been, searching for a pressure point. "You're okay, hon, you're okay," she soothed, holding him down while I yanked the car back and forth, trying to upset the chopper's aim, which began to throw up great columns of highway and dirt right next to us. The road twisted, keeping him from having too much time with us in his sights.

Then Pam left Wellman and took the other Magnum out of her backpack. "Steve, don't slam on the brakes, but slow down fast around the next turn, and maybe I can use this police iron on him." She squirmed up into the back window, knocked out some larger splinters in her way, and, holding the pistol in both hands, waited to sight on the chopper. I slowed us down as suddenly as I could, and the chopper, coming around the turn behind us, lagged our moves a little, narrowing the gap. Pam's pistol boomed away. In the outside mirror I could see Plexiglas flake out of the right side of the Cobra; then it soared upward, flew a graceful wingover, and dropped into the pines upside down. A moment later a fireball rose from the woods. "Wish Chester'd been aboard," I said.

"Me too," Pam replied. The strings that let her kill were going slack; she had a gray, shocked look now.

"You're some lifeguard, lady."

She nodded, wanting not to be with us for a time.

"That's why Chester made it so easy for us," Dunham said. "So the chopper could pop us. What now?"

"Hospital for Wellman," I said. "Then a night's sleep and some heavy writing. Then we're off to New Mexico."

Pam looked up wearily. "There's more?"

"Just a bit."

"But you're doing the story now?" Dunham wanted to know.

"You kidding? Of course I am."

"Will the agency have a chance to say anything about *Brideshead?*"

"Like what? Brave NASA scientists jailed for misappropriation of funds? Somehow I don't see that one clearing your internal review, Les."

"Steve, since we're blood brothers and all, give me a couple of days on this one."

"Jesus, man, we've got the whole fucking government trying to kill us, and you begin to think about how your agency's going to *look*." I shook my head vigorously. "Hell, no, I'm filing in the morning."

"I'm not trying to hush anything up, Steve. I'm really not. But there's big security problems with this. Christ, we've got a dead cosmonaut in one of our spacecraft. We've got our whole shuttle program smeared with this heavy military involvement. We've got all this government killing going down. We've got a civilian spacecraft turned into an intelligence ploy that was a goddamned act of war. The President needs to know. The Congress."

"And the parish priest," I added sarcastically, knowing he was right, reluctant to yield. "The sooner we get this out where a few million souls know about it, the sooner they'll stop trying to hit us. I've finally got the puzzle pretty much together, so they really *need* to hit me, along with everybody else. You. Pam. Wellman. God knows who-all. Survival tells me I have to file."

"If you didn't have to corroborate something in New Mexico, you wouldn't be going. You *can't* file yet."

"I can."

"Just give me the time it takes you to get to New Mexico and do whatever you need to do. We've got a little jump on them now. Give me until you get what you need out there. A day or two."

"That'd be gambling on how much ahead of them we are, Les. I've been wrong every goddamned time I've tried to estimate my lead. It's always been shorter than I would've believed."

"I gambled coming down here with you. Gamble with me on this. Maybe I can get better results going up through government than you can going public. Let's try for some results, okay?"

"Okay."

We went through the Arsenal gate without stopping, driving our shot-up machine as if it didn't have a rear end full of bullet holes. The young man there said something but didn't shoot, and then we were on the freeway, booming north toward Huntsville and some medical help for Wellman. "How's he doing?" I asked Pam.

She shook her head where I could see it in the mirror and said, "Bad shock, Steve."

I looked over the seat. The old man had gone very gray, shivering with the inner cold his blood couldn't warm up for him. "Les, when we get him there I'd like you to stay with him. For one thing, you've got those gunshot wounds to explain."

"I'll get him settled. Then I'm off to D.C. to do my thing."

We began to pick up blue hospital signs along the interstate and followed them into town and traffic, where we bulled through traffic lights and wrong-wayed one-way streets. After an eternity of town we reached the emergency ramp at Huntsville Hospital and turned in and got stopped and the doors open. Dunham hurried in for help, and Pam and I shifted the old man around some, in the hope of easing him out. While we were doing this, he lifted his terribly aged head and, in a whisper I could barely hear, said, "Vait, Mr. Borg . . . vait . . . I think . . . I tell you about *Godfoot.*"

PART THREE

"Mr. Borg, here is a cultural note for you. I find the quality of American agents is deteriorating. I also find they use their worst people in scientific operations. What do you think of that?"

1

Pam wouldn't let us stay near Huntsville, even with fatigue drawing us like a hypnotist toward sleep, even with our minds jumpy with the pantomimes of killing, which still rehearsed within. So instead of a Huntsville motel we drove our torn-up rental car back to Pryor, left it at the field with some talk of Uncle Sam's accident and two hundred dollars, and flew the Cardinal another hour west, until we came to little West Helena, south of Memphis, where the big river meanders crazily through flat, black, haze-bound lands. And there, in a John Garfield–style motel on the airport side of town, Pam fell into sleep while I rubbed the smooth, lightly furred contours of her back, sending thumbs and fingers along shoulder blades and spine, waiting for fatigue to let me follow her.

The noises of killing still echoed across my mind, the plop-plop of the chopper, the booming of its cannon rounds, so that I had to reduce the volume, force myself to focus somewhere else. And, in that mode, for the first time in a couple of days, I thought of Cerf, grizzly eyes, aura of great cruelty, his giving me the three terms. I wondered how many of them he'd understood.

Wellman had spent longer than was good for him talking about *Godfoot,* telling me little I hadn't figured out at that point, but having to tell it. He had talked and I had listened, while they lay him on the wheeled table, while they wheeled him in; he talked until the morphine made him sleep and unlocked the small gray hand that gripped my sleeve as though it must hang on to it forever.

He said that when they'd been planning the shuttle program, in the very early days when all they'd had really was an idea and some Buck Rogers sketches of the ship, someone had raised the problem of a lethal accident, a disabled spacecraft. It hadn't been like Skylab, which was just a hundred-foot-long, furnished fuel tank, structurally unable to survive reentry even marginally intact. And Skylab had been clean—there were no reactors, no pumped-up lasers, on Skylab. So all that one sent back to earth were shards and fragments, all scattered across the southern ocean and Australia.

Shuttle would be different, the worst-case argument ran. Designed to survive reentry, it would pose a real hazard if it returned uncontrolled. If it hit a city it would be like a DC–9 crashing at top speed, a kind of bomb even then. Still, they reasoned, it would be no worse than that kind of crash. A tolerable risk. Moreover, there had also been a feeling that looking ahead that far, in a country where money came a year at a time, was just borrowing trouble. Hell, by then, if something disabled a shuttle, there'd be a way to boost it farther out or bring it in over the ocean.

The countercurrents had come mainly from John Chester and a couple of other engineers, who, stimulated by the idea of a crippled shuttle returning to the surface, began to argue for more control over the situation. As Wellman put it, the longer they talked, the better the possibilities became. Their ideas coalesced into a plot, the plot into a project. Perhaps the ship could be rigged for a demand reentry, to come back at a time and place we could always determine from the ground. And, pleading the fuck-up and citing unusual solar activity perhaps, they could use the reentry to force something—at the time no one even knew what they wanted—out of the Russians. The advent of Soviet killer-satellite technology had given them an ideal motive: The Russians would have to demonstrate how much, or how little, satellite-killing capability they really had to keep the falling spacecraft away from one of their cities.

To Wellman and his colleagues, the whole thing had sounded blue sky and sick; they turned away from bombarding civilians with debris from space in the name of national intelligence. But somebody apparently liked the idea, for it had been code-named *Godfoot* and quickly classified, which, in a civilian agency like NASA, was something like having the project die. Wellman told me he'd thought *Godfoot* was just paper until we heard that *Excalibur* would reenter over Kiev. "That vas vhy they let us go, Mr. Borg. Only the four of us knew there *vas a Godfoot*. They are trying to keep qviet an act of var."

Well, I continued, tempting sleep, they'd begun with the idea that people might die in the Kiev footprint. Once they'd opted for the killer-satellite demonstration, it became important enough to murder for. And more. They were, as the old man said, covering up an act of war against the Soviet Union. They had the virginity of a civilian space program to protect. And then I thought how it must have gone, really, with no straight thinking about actions and consequences, but instead the growth of momentum you get in any government project that lasts too long. They'd had this program under way for all those years, with nothing happening: Then chance had given them a fatal accident aboard *Excalibur* and a derelict armed as a virtual nuclear bomb. Now they could spring the big surprise on Mother Russia. When Dunham had told Chester I wanted to talk about a six-year-old code name, when I had intimated to him that I knew about a clandestine operation and might blow it just as its succulent fruits were about to drop, I could imagine it causing conferences, problems. I could see them shaking their heads sadly over a half-acre table at Langley. The killer-satellite demo would shape our defense for a generation to come, and you couldn't cook omelettes without breaking eggs, and nothing must stop old *Godfoot,* not even Steve Borg and his little entourage of endangered species. So, by their standards, they'd started cheap, wasting Marcia accidentally. And then, trapped into killing, worried that *Godfoot* might yet pop loose, they escalated to the airliner bombing, then went for Pam and me in the Cardinal, and, finally, insanely, sent out John Chester and the bully boys. All to protect *Godfoot.*

But, I inserted here, drawing new data from my soft, tired brain, Danilov had known about *Godfoot.* The Russians had known about it and mounted a counterproject that must have been called *Kiev Centre.* Wellman, beginning to sink under the morphine, had tried to laugh when I told him the name, saying, "Ah, that sounds an excellent Soviet codename." And Danilov, I thought now, Danilov hadn't wanted spooks in either camp to contaminate the grand neutrality of space; he'd been dirtied, maybe by John Chester, and afterward decided to cultivate me, feed it to me so I could write it up, kill it with light. He'd gone to *Excalibur* carrying explosives, the cosmonaut sapper of his poem. And something had gone sour and marooned him up there, but not before he fixed things so Russia could have produced a mind-boggling, but false, demonstration of how well their killer satellite worked. Except he'd also undone his mining before he ran out of air. *Excalibur* hadn't blown up; it had simply reentered.

Both sides had the intelligence coup of a lifetime working on that reentry, but then *Godfoot* hadn't been allowed to happen, or *Kiev Centre* either. Nobody who counted on either side had known about *Brideshead,* which had dissolved all their intentions, without regard to race or national origin. The *Godfoot* people and the *Kiev Centre* people were still out there, armed and considered dangerous; they would want to pop us. They would always want to, as long as our silence meant total silence. I felt pursued once more, at bay, frightened by the endlessness of the goddamned pursuit, which seemed to reach down through me forever, to everyone I touched.

Maybe, I thought, grasping for some reason for the bureaucracy to leave us alone, maybe the four of us can fall through an operational crack and cease to be important to the agency. Maybe, what with *Godfoot* failed, they would be eager to get on with more successful work. Except they had no way of knowing about *Kiev Centre.* They might still believe they had a secret they could keep. Telling them the Russians knew about *Godfoot* and promising silence might quiet them down. Except I didn't intend to promise anybody my silence. And I sensed that, once killing began, it was impossible to turn off until all the killing had been done.

And how about the *Kiev Centre* side? Their project hadn't happened either. Would they think we'd detected their lost cosmonaut? Mightn't they want to silence those who'd seen Danilov's anguished face from his big space-borne coffin? Sure they would.

Cerf would. You get shot at by Tweedledum, and Tweedledee comes around mopping up.

Frightened and despairing, my mind began shutting down, finally ready for sleep. I thought, as I lay like a spoon against Pam's back, that we would probably awaken in a room full of civil servants in silk and blue serge suits and that I'd ask them my new, purely rhetorical question: Who told the Russians about *Godfoot?*

And give them my purely rhetorical answer: Sonya Van Deer.

I still thought I knew it all.

2

Pam dreamed like a pointer all night, legs reflexing, the face telling a dread and silent story. I did no better, spending the night anxiously in search of identity and sense, on assignment in unknown cities, calling my mother and getting Cerf.

We had breakfast near the motel, where, among the ham and eggs and grits and canned orange juice, I searched the Memphis *Commerical Appeal* for an *Excalibur* reentry story and found nothing; it had missed the morning papers, then.

Not long after dawn we climbed away from West Helena, the day beginning to heat up as the sun ascended behind us, turning the western purple the color of sand. Once we stopped for fuel at Duncan, Oklahoma, and got some crackers and a Coke from the machines; and then we went our way, staying within five hundred feet of the terrain, the red clay and little hills of that state shading into the shale and sand of the Texas Panhandle, the earth rising to meet us as it sloped toward the Divide. The sun overtook us as we traded the rich green of the irrigated lands south of Lubbock for the brown, overgrazed stubble of eastern New Mexico, from which we could see the moonscape mountains of the southwest trembling in the distance.

She and I scarcely spoke. So much had gone down that it had left us numb. I kept my hand on her thigh, she now and then put hers on mine, and we forged along, drinking the ennui of a long flight in a little plane as an antidote for killing. I thought about Dunham, half-missed him, wondered if he'd caught his plane for

Washington, or got one out last night, or what, and how he was doing on this "inside."

The reentry story caught up to us not long after the sun did. Every hour through the trip I'd tuned the ADF to radio stations along our line of flight. The noon news out of Roswell had a short wire-service story about the reentry that told us how, hours after the White House had announced *Excalibur* would rain down on Kiev, NASA technicians in Huntsville had managed to gain control of the derelict satellite and force it down into the South Pacific. And that was it. Dunham's bullshit, I decided. And . . . maybe . . . it was over.

And, in fact, nothing seemed to pursue us. The contiguous military-operations areas on the charts fielded their jets without ramming us; no controller came on the flight-watch frequency to tell us lies, steer us into a mountain; and nobody questioned the phony numbers Pam used on the radio, demonstrating that it's still a rather free country, even when flying. Maybe, I thought, they've lost interest. I began to share the thought with Pam but couldn't; to speak of it would alert some primitive god, who would restore the interest of governments and see us hounded to death. So I held my silence, hoping what I sensed was correct.

Below us, the grazed-out ranch lands gave way to tank farms and derricks and birdlike pumps sipping oil, and the tank farms to an unpitted moon, and the moon to the little sterile grid of Roswell, and Roswell to mountains that swam slowly toward us like whales in an ocean of sand. Then we were drifting over the complex folds of the Sacramento Mountains—broad, flattened pleats of pine-covered rock, anomalously cool in this sun-blasted land. Off to the west the further accident of White Sands glittered against another stone leviathan, and ancient black lava flowed north across the desert, lava out of nothing into nothing. It evoked a slip of God's hand, this odd mix of rounded mountains, lava, and foam-colored sand.

Alamo Peak Observatory leaped at us from its pined hiding place, like ruins in the jungle, the enormous vacuum-tower telescope rising white and pristine as a sacrificial platform from the pines and scrub oaks, the other monolithic, domed structures gathered nearby, with the smaller rectangles of administration and residence buildings nearly hidden from us, even when we soared close to the folded ridges. Pam brought us around in a wide circle low enough that the rough air flowing across the mountain jarred us intermittently. We took it in, trying to memorize this new turf that looked so like a temple to the sun. I said, "That's it," and she gave me a look that said we shared the sense of the observatory being a kind of terminus for us. The sense and the dread of it.

Then she pulled back the power and dropped the wheels, keeping the engine warm through an ear-popping descent over the western slope of the mountains and the little desert grid of Alamogordo and into an airport where Flying Fortresses and Neptunes and Liberators, kept alive to carry flame-retardant chemicals, rusty red with the carrying of them, lined the taxiways. The voice on the Unicom told us to park anywhere except the first space, and she shut down the Cardinal and we got out, decelerating, becoming folks again in the vibrating stillness that follows a long haul in a small plane. The sun beat like a heart overhead; nothing moved in the harsh, hot light.

And nothing seemed to pursue us. We both felt it. "Maybe," I began, but I couldn't say it for all the bad luck the uttering of it would bring. Pam only shook her head, peering like a hunter through the long-vistaed heat of this desert land.

I got an afternoon Albuquerque *Tribune*, and we went into the restaurant where a fat girl who ate more than she cooked sold us some coffee and frozen pie; and we worked on that, and looked into one another's eyes, and wondered how and whether we'd get back in touch after all we'd shared. Then I searched the paper for more on *Excalibur* and found a pageful of wire-service prose about the reentry, the Huntsville Group, how the reentry looked to sailors, and this red-boxed bulletin:

MYSTERY EXPLOSION SLAYS SHUTTLE TEAM

Huntsville, Alabama, August 15.—In a cruel twist of fate, the handful of men and women who yesterday saved the world from the debris of a reentering space shuttle were killed only hours later by a mysterious explosion that leveled the center from which they controlled the reentry.

The 100-ton shuttle *Excalibur* had been in a decaying orbit for some time, following an accident early in its mission that killed the four astronauts aboard. Early yesterday, the National Aeronautics and Space Administration had announced that the derelict spacecraft, one of the largest objects ever placed in orbit, would reenter debris along a "footprint" centered on the Russian city of Kiev.

But the Huntsville team of space scientists, in an effort the space agency had kept secret, managed to regain control of *Excalibur* and cause it to reenter harmlessly over the South Pacific Ocean.

According to a space-agency spokesman, the team of scientists at the Marshall Space Flight Center here had been scheduled to fly to Washington today to accept their agency's highest award for their lifesaving efforts.

Military authorities from Huntsville Arsenal at the scene of the explosion said it appeared old ammunition buried beneath the building had spontaneously detonated. The building, according to Army sources, had formerly been used to handle heavy artillery shells.

A "massive safety program" was being launched, they said, to find any other buried ammunition that might be a "time bomb" in the NASA facilities here.

While Marshall Center authorities withheld the names of those killed in yesterday's explosion, it was known that Dr. Brendan James, 48, the English scientist long-associated with the shuttle program, was among the fatalities.

The sole survivor of the explosion, Dr. Helmut Wellman, 68, died of injuries received in the blast at Huntsville Hospital. . . .

"Jesus," I whispered. "Oh, Jesus Christ." Another roomful of people were gone, were murdered. I knew they'd been murdered as surely as I knew anything. The killing went on. Somehow, they'd blown up the Huntsville Group. Somehow, they'd moved in on old Wellman in the hospital and pulled the plug on him, too. And now we could feel pursued again, as they fanned out to murder everyone who knew they murdered, everyone who knew they lied. I felt alone and fear touched my insides. I passed the paper to Pam, saying, "Look at that," and while she read I used my *Herald* credit card to call Dunham, the other trusted person in our shrinking universe of friendly people.

When his secretary came on I asked for Les. She hesitated and then said, "Mr. Dunham won't be in today."

"I'll try him at home, then," I replied, hating this barrier.

"Are you a friend of his, sir?"

"Yes," I said, remembering that his daughter had asked me the same question two nights ago.

"Well . . . he's had a serious accident." Her voice shifted from neutral to concerned. "Very serious."

The skin on my neck moved. I thought of good-byes to daughters. "What happened?"

"On his way in this morning . . ."

"From home?"

"Yes, he came back from Huntsville last night."

Good, I thought. He saw his girl again. "Where is he now?"

"A big truck just brushed him right off the road. He's at Bethesda," she went on, reminding me Dunham had been in the Navy, "in critical condition . . ."

For some reason the bland description powerfully evoked the dying Dunham, the monkey face, pale gray and gasping, the eyes unseeing, the brain unable to run its usual race, the limbs and fingers dancing now and then to random stimuli, all in a veinous forest of tubes beneath a fluorescent sun . . . But I rallied then and said, "That's terrible news. But, look, the reason I called was about his story on the accident in Huntsville."

"The explosion?" Her voice had a worried note now.

"Yes. I'm Nick Carter with the *Journal*, and there were a couple questions." I'd begun to feel like Nick Carter. "So I wanted to talk to Les about it."

"Well, it wasn't his story, Mr., uh, Carter."

"Whose was it?"

"The AP wrote it in Huntsville."

"But it mentions a NASA spokesman."

"Oh, that'd be John Chester. He's down there right now, and I guess he just stepped in. But he's not in public affairs. He's an engineer."

"I guess I know John."

"Do you want his extension?"

"No, I've got his number, thanks." I put the phone back in

its cradle, leaned against the smeared chromium of the machine. I've got his number. He's got mine. He's taken care of Wellman. Now he'll be coming after us. Yes, and they, the other they, got old Dunham and probably that roomful of people in Huntsville. I watched Pam, who seemed nervous, and went over to her and told her about Dunham, which made tears stand in her eyes until she shut them and turned away as though she was through looking at me. "Hard times, lady. These are hard times indeed." She nodded with a motion that said: Go away.

I went back to the phone and dialed the *Herald*. When Rosie (our lady of the switchboard) answered I didn't say howdy or anything; I asked for the news editor. She put me through to a voice I didn't recognize until it said, "Wilson."

"Terry," I said, "It's Steve Borg."

"Steve. Jesus, where are you?"

"Tell you some other time, Terry. Horatio there?" I had in mind using Horatio as my link into the system, which he apparently understood, since he gave me the lethal airline tickets; and I was keyed up, jumpy, waiting for my chance to talk directly to one of the BFE's troops.

"You don't know?"

"Know?" My stomach began to know, though. Time was river on the flood, and my instincts had hardened enough to discriminate immediately between the trees it brought me and the bodies. Now I saw Horatio's sweep toward me. "What happened?"

"He got mugged. You know, he liked to eat down on calle ocho, and he was down there too late last night and some guys mugged him. Sign of age, Steve, when a pack of punks decides they might as well take you. Anyway, they beat in his head and took his money. I covered it. Happens all night long in Miami."

"Jesus."

"People keep trying to find out where you are, Steven. Your mom. People. I'm not asking, on account of I understand your problem."

"Horatio understood my problem, Terry. And he helped them make a try at me. But they still took him out."

"Something to watch out for, Steve, is when one pass is made at you you begin to think you're the reason they invented death. Want to talk?"

"No." I let my end of the line go silent for a moment, thinking: They're listening. Can't let Terry know very much, or they'll waste him too. But, shit, put their surveillance to work for you. Think poker. So I said, "Really can't, Terry. But I could use some insurance. I've got a hell of a story written on the *Excalibur* thing and on some peculiar foreign connections. I want to send the story to you. Don't read it. Just put it in the safest place you know, where even the fucking government can't read it. Okay?"

"Sure, Steve." Maybe they'd got to him too. I listened hard to see if I could detect the slightest tremor. He seemed solid.

"Thanks."

"Sure."

Returning to Pam, I said, "Horatio was killed by muggers in Miami."

"Who's Horatio?"

"My old editor." It made me sad to say it. Horatio, I thought, I forgive you for that plane ticket.

"So they're still after us." Her voice carried a deep vein of despair. She closed her eyes, like a lover showing pain.

"They still are. Everybody is. It isn't just Chester's gang now. Somebody's going around mopping up from the other side."

"Jesus."

"Maybe I got us some insurance, though." I told her about Terry Wilson and what I said I'd send. "The possibility of publishing what we have might make them lay low." I felt in my deep bowel that I might be willing to sell some silence after all.

"Nothing's written."

"All I need to do is send Terry a package. He won't read it."

"Sure he won't." But her eyes had lighted up again. She was back in combat. "Best we get moving, babe."

We rented an Avis Aspen from a young lady from Mexico. While the Wizard did his thing, my eye wandered to a taxiing

Frontier flight, a turboprop Convair that trundled up, opened its clam shell, and dispensed farm folk and Indians, service people and cowboys. When Cerf came through the door I felt his cruelty, even at that distance. He exited in his blazer and light slacks, still dressed for selling cars but large and deadly, stooped slightly with the false humility of a trained bear. "Pam," I said, "we gotta go."

She looked quickly toward the transport. "Him?" She'd seen the grizzly eyes.

3

At some point, maybe back over the sluggish rivers of the Southeast, but somewhere, I'd seen our drive up to Alamo Peak Observatory as the cleansing of a detail, the completion of a neat knot. But now we seemed to be fleeing to those solar temples, sensing the two sides ranging across our trail, herding us into the desert mountains under a blaze of sunlight.

So we traveled frightened but without a stampede. We stopped at the post office and mailed Terry Wilson some page-sized sheets torn from the Albuquerque *Journal* in a lavishly stapled Jiffy bag, sent it registered and special delivery, to put it in Miami within the month. Then we found a sporting-goods store, where Pam ran in and bought ammunition for her .38 and the two government Magnums she'd taken off the agents in Gaithersburg. As we hurried up the mountain she poked the rounds into the cylinder of the pistol she'd used on the chopper, and I laughed and said, "Well, Bonnie."

And she laughed back, "Well, *well*, Clyde," and we each put a hand on the other's thigh, which was how we rode around together.

I pushed the softly suspended Aspen around the ascending turns like a rusty pro, with the hot, dry dust-laden air pumping into the car, and pines appearing suddenly along the road as our ascent took us to a kinder climate. While we drove my mind ran some circles of its own, shuffling our options now that we knew who the enemy—the enemies, at this point—were. Cerf still lagged us. Chester was still back east someplace, trying to find the trail. They hovered in my mind, vividly lethal, stalking us from different sides. Maybe. . . . "Maybe they'll cancel each other out," I said.

"Who?" Pam returned from some mental distance.

"Cerf, the Russian. And Chester, whom you've met."

"If they do, the powers'll just send out a fresh squad."

"I don't know. Cerf's a long way from home. Maybe he's got a lot of autonomy. Maybe if something happens to him we just become an unknown wild card, and the bureaucracy forgets us. The same might be true of Chester. They know he's after somebody. What if they don't know who, or why?"

"What if?" Again, her voice carried that note of despair. "Maybe we just run and run until they get us, Steve."

"I don't like that one."

"Me neither. But it sure God looks that way from here."

"Yeah, but . . ." My conviction sagged. "When we open this up, they'll *have* to leave us alone. I mean, the goddamned *President* will know about it."

"What makes you think he doesn't?"

"It can't stand light," I said. "If we light it up, they have to go away."

"Until the lights go out," Pam countered. "Like Dracula."

"Where's my old runnin' gun?"

"Sorry."

"We shall overcome."

"Sure."

A sign at Cloudcroft turned us south, to weave across what passed for the broad back and shoulder blades of the massif through the sharp light of nine thousand feet. Soon we could see the vacuum-tower telescope poking up through the pines, and finally a sign steered us off the highway to Alamo Peak Observatory, the blacktop taking us to a gate guarded by a white civilian in the black pants and blue western-cut shirt and billed cap of all guards and the mean, red-neck face and amber shades of the rural-cop archetype. He waved us down and thrust a map of the observatory grounds at me, then let us enter.

We drove past a scatter of frame homes, gray-green government-issue bungalows that ran back in among the pines, and a couple of white cement structures the map said housed the main labs, administrative offices, and computer. We put the car in the parking lot and got out on the blacktop, where I fired a couple of frames with the Nikon. The observatory buildings loomed, templelike, the white tower at one end of a circular drive, with domed buildings around the circle, all peering through cracked hemispheres and telescopes at the sun. The stellar object of all this worship trembled in the southwestern sky, unbearably bright, the harsh shards of its light shattering where they flew through the trees. One felt the distant violence of our star.

Sonya Van Deer wasn't in the little group of lumberjack-shirted astronomers and technicians in the main lab building, but a pretty Mexican receptionist there, after making a couple of calls, told us she could be found in the tower building. She pointed redundantly toward the ten-story structure that rose through the trees across the loop, graceful as an extended wing, smoothly monolithic, as though the narrow pyramidal edifice had been shaved out of soapstone.

Up close it was less so; one saw the doors and seams, the residual touch of human hands. We followed the signs into the glass doors and a lobby where exhibits explained the facility and a closed-circuit television screen showed us the sun in hydrogen-alpha light. It looked angry.

I saw her then, still the beautiful violinist seen at a distance, a person to make the heart leap, in an observing room off to the right. She wore Levi's and running shoes and a light shirt, through which her breasts were silhouetted by the light behind her. Her braid was intact. I must have emitted a scent, for Pam looked sharply at me, frowned, and looked away when I caught her. "Come on," I said.

Van Deer didn't see us come up or notice that I photographed her, but continued to play the controls on a console under a scarlet hydrogen-alpha image of the sun nearly two feet across. At that size, in that color, the star looked incredibly stormy, even by solar standards; you could sense its immense reach out through space. "Looks mean," I said, coming up behind her. It made her jump and turn quickly toward me.

"I . . ." she said, giving me the look of a former lover wondering who the hell I was.

"Steve Borg, Dr. Van Deer. From the Miami *Herald*."

"Oh, I remember, of course."

"And Pamela Rudd."

"How do you do?" I couldn't tell whether our astronomer was relieved it was just us or troubled that something unforeseen had happened. If one thing had, others might. Scientists like predictables, even when they're breaking new ground.

"We're looking the place over," I said.

"Good, can I help?" She offered help to pay us for the relief she felt. A funny, obvious woman, this Sonya Van Deer.

"Well, can you tell us something about the telescope here?"

So she did. She said the tower telescope used a vacuum to help astronomers get a clear view of the sun, which was a problem because sunlight normally heats the air in a telescope tube, blurring the solar image. "The whole building is an instrument," she went on, disappearing into her science like a small mammal into a burrow.

I recalled her. "I remember your paper in Miami. Something about unusually high levels of solar activity, which you'd predicted using the techniques of the Soviet scientist Andreev."

"Your memory is very good, Mr. Borg."

"I broke the *Excalibur* reentry story."

"That's right, I remember." She faltered, then headed for her burrow. "Because we have this long vacuum telescope, we can observe extremely small features in the sun's surface and lower atmosphere."

"Of course, there was never any question of the sun's really affecting *Excalibur*."

She shook her head like someone dreaming. "In fact," she said, "the orbit has been greatly curtailed by our present high level of activity, Mr. Borg." Then, quickly, "In here, we control the telescope and its spectrographs and other instruments through a small computer. And the entire tower . . ."

"Given *Godfoot*, I mean. Given *Godfoot*, *Excalibur* could be brought in anytime."

"I don't know what this *Godfoot* is, Mr. Borg." Relief fled her voice. Now it was offense as the best defense.

"Yes you do. Want to talk?"

"I've nothing to say to the press."

"Then say something to us. Everybody's been trying to kill us over this, Doc. They'll keep at me until I write something."

"I've nothing to say." But her voice shrank rapidly. "To continue . . . the entire tower, including this observing room, is suspended near the top of the tower by a mercury-float bearing, so that we can rotate the image of the sun by rotating the instrument, which . . ."

"I made an interesting Gestalt," I told her. "The Van Deer to Andreev anagram came to me in a vision."

". . . which turns out to be the whole building," she shrilled, unable to look at me now.

"Andreev is your father."

Her voice rose a quarter-octave. "This is one of the best-resolved solar images in existence."

"The Russians have your father."

"My father is *dead*." Cornered, she began to turn, emphasizing the last word, perhaps to give us some sense of her freedom, having him free of Russia. I don't know.

"You had to work for them."

"No."

"You told them about *Godfoot*."

"No." Not exclaimed, merely said.

"Listen, both sides are liquidating their witnesses. Our side. The Russian side."

"That has nothing to do with me."

"You think because your father's dead you're free. You're not."

"No." But her will began to break. She heard the same footsteps we did; she knew how it went when the killing started. I kept silence long enough to let her work out what she wanted to say. Finally, she whispered, "My father is dead. Boris Alexandrovich Andreev is dead. They've killed him."

"I'm sorry."

"I didn't tell them about *Godfoot*. They told me." She looked at us with tears standing in her pale eyes. My knees trembled. Pam saw me go soft and sneered. "Let's walk outside," said Sonya Van Deer.

And when we were a threesome strolling the loop with a score of other visitors, she said, "They knew about *Godfoot*. They had a plan . . ."

"They put Vladimir Danilov into the shuttle with explosive charges they could set off from the ground. But Vlad got stuck . . ."

"Vladimir?" I sensed my old friend had untied her braid in Geneva. "I knew he died, but . . ."

"At Huntsville we saw him, his body, floating in *Excalibur*."

"God."

"A bad way to die." And there are men after us with worse ways in their kits.

She said, "Once they'd put explosives aboard the shuttle, they needed some insurance against NASA's sending up another mission to visit *Excalibur*. They approached me . . ."

"Through your father, in Geneva."

"Yes. They wanted me to expand the official U.S. prediction of solar activity. A very active sun would mean there wouldn't be time to get to *Excalibur*. NASA would stop trying. In exchange, my father could get out perhaps."

"So you raised the level of predicted solar activity, in Miami."

"I did."

"And Cerf was there to watch you, to make sure it took?"

She nodded.

"And I helped," I said, drawing a tired smile from her. "But now they're killing off everyone involved. Your father, us, you, everybody."

"Will they be after me?" It had an egocentered sound in our present situation, a kind of How come they're after me when they can have you? sound. I thought: In a pinch she'll sell you fast, man.

"They're killing everybody," I said.

"Ah, well, if they come, they come. Meanwhile, I do my work." She was shitting us. Pam radiated her sense of it, too.

"There's no exit," I said. "They really will come. They really will pop you, even if you helped them. Your father helped them. Where is he?"

"Dead. My father is dead." It crushed her back into line, remembering her father.

"Don't you believe it?"

"No, it's true, they killed him. But they owe me a little. I think they might leave me alone."

"Maybe they would have. Maybe not. Certainly not when they find you've seen me again and we've talked privately. I have the true Judas kiss, lady."

"He does," Pam said. "If there's one thing he's got, it's his Judas kiss." I'd been kidding; she wasn't and gave me a hard look back when I glanced my surprise.

"Thanks," I said.

"Sorry," Pam said. "This running's wearing me down." Her voice was gentle, but her face said she was falling out of love.

Van Deer intruded with, "What do you suggest, Mr. Borg?"

"I don't know. I don't know how far behind us they are."

"About a minute and a half," Pam said.

"We saw Cerf at the airport," I told Van Deer. "He's right behind us." I let her look stricken and added, "He's not bringing you a paycheck."

"I know."

"He's not even that far, hon," Pam said.

I looked where she was looking and saw Cerf among a little tangle of tourists in the parking lot, the grinning bear, watching us with grizzly eyes.

4

Cerf held us there, it seemed, through an effort of will. He padded toward us on his bowed boxer's legs, his head weaving slightly from side to side in time to his gait. Sonya Van Deer wavered, strongly drawn, like an iron filing feeling a magnetic field; you could sense her stirring, wanting to go to Cerf, throw herself on his mercy, sell us if she could, but survive. If there had been the faintest light of human kindness in his cavernous, angry eyes, she would have broken cover like a bird. And *still* she might have gone to him if I hadn't restrained her gently with a hand on her uncovered upper arm. The sharp reality of this first touch of my distant violinist disconcerted me, weakened my concentration. I couldn't look at Pam, and hours later I still felt Sonya's warm, taut skin beneath my fingers.

I tried to concentrate on the advancing juggernaut. My hand wrapped around the Magnum in my windbreaker pocket. Pam had her pocketed .38 in hand. Huntsville had been a watershed: Combat confused us less now; we just went for our guns, ready to use them. Cerf saw our loaded pockets and seemed to understand we'd use them if spooked. So he came on softly, with a cordial, gold-toothed grin, saying, "Mr. Borg, how nice to see you again." I nodded. "And the charming Pamela Rudd, I believe," he went on, "and Doctor Van Deer."

"Sounds like you know everybody," I said.

"I do." He broadened his big, carnivorous grin. "How are you coming with your puzzle, Mr. Borg?"

"I guess I have it all."

"You have nothing like all of it, but perhaps you understand enough to know that Sonya and I are colleagues. I must see her for a while in private."

I felt her reflex toward him and held her back. He radiated death. Still spinning the illusion that I could keep Cerf from having his way, I said, "No." She just looked at me, did nothing, hoped it would come out all right. Her acceptance of her situation puzzled me, but peripherally; all my attention focused on Cerf.

"You have to understand also, Mr. Borg, that Sonya is not a strong-willed person. She is beautiful, which makes one think her will is good too. But in fact it is quite weak."

And still she said nothing, but leaned toward him like a plant. I said, "But she's staying with us."

"As you wish. Have you done any writing lately, Mr. Borg?" Cerf held his reasonable tone, but his face had grown crimson and ugly with anger.

"Enough. I've bought a little time."

"I think you already have that. A little time."

"More than you think."

"Oh, I doubt it." He glowered for a moment, trying to will Sonya away from us. Then, seeing no movement from her, he smiled in imitation of regret, shook his head, and said, "Another time, then, Sonya. I'm sure there will be another time, Mr. Borg."

I said, "I know, I know," and Pam and I steered Sonya Van Deer away from this hulking danger, as though he threatened only her. There was something magnetic about her weakness. She made no protest, not even when we'd cleared the entrance gate and were hurrying toward Cloudcroft, but only stared evenly ahead, beautiful in her trance, and frightened as a bird who's spoken to a snake, and cold.

Nothing followed us, at least nothing within view.

When we'd turned toward Alamogordo and the mountain road snaked down to the desert ahead of us, Sonya said, like someone back from amnesia picking up an old conversational thread, "Do you have a plan?"

"Sure," I said. "Plan X."

Pam laughed, but it had a bitter sound to it.

Sonya said, "I need information, not jokes. I don't flee into the desert with strangers, Mr. Borg."

"Don't get tough with me, Doc. I've seen you in action."

She curled her lip and turned away.

"Want to hear Plan X?" I asked.

She nodded, sulking.

"I've got a friend in Santa Fe. Randy Jones . . ."

"Randy and I are old friends."

"I forgot."

"Will she protect you?"

"Us. Sure. It'll give me time to get my story written and filed with the *Herald*. Once they run it, everybody'll begin leaving us alone. We can surface."

"I'm not stopping at Santa Fe, Steve," Pam put in. This was the bomb she'd been wanting to drop all afternoon.

It surprised me, made my stomach hurt. "I thought we were going through this together."

"We were. But it's started getting me down. It just goes on and on. And it's getting kind of crowded. I'll take you two to Santa Fe, then I guess I'll split."

"Don't leave on my account, Miss Rudd," Sonya said. "I don't plan to compete with you for Mr. Borg."

"Thanks a heap. Fact is, I'm a working girl and best get back to it."

"I wish you wouldn't," I said.

She nodded, lowered her eyelids.

"They'll come after you, Pam."

"They will anyway, hon. I may swing way south or something. We'll see." Then, "Don't worry."

"I do worry. I want you around."

"I think going to Randy is a good idea, Mr. Borg," the even, passive, passionless voice intruded. "A good idea."

"Good." But it pissed me off, to have this mere braid of a person and to be losing my Pam. I looked at her and felt the breach widen between us in the silence beyond our little burst of conversation, a silence that persisted all the way back to the field at Alamogordo.

We returned the car to Avis and Pam paid her fuel bill, and we boarded the Cardinal while she did her preflight, Sonya sitting in back. In a few minutes Pam was aboard, and the little engine hammered away in the heat. Again, Pam and I shared, in a glance, that sense of being unpursued. But it was mere illusion. As we taxied past the little terminal building, Cerf waddled out to watch us and waved. I waved back, but my heart wasn't in it.

She had her checklist done by the time we were ready to turn onto the runway, looked around for traffic, and began her takeoff run even while she got the airplane lined up. With full tanks and a third person and our belongings the Cardinal was heavy in the high, hot air and got off like a Doolittle bomber clearing the bow of the *Wasp*. For a time we wallowed along, while she got the wheels and flaps up. Then the plane accelerated and she let it climb, steering us out over the desert south of the monolith, the observatory wheeling past above us to the north. After getting a response from flight service, she said, "Cardinal three-four-five-one-six, Albuquerque, we're VFR from Alamogordo to Miami, Florida, and I'd like you to open our flight plan at two-five past the hour." They said they would and she put the mike away.

"You're laying down a trail," I said.

"We'll let them have a few hours of it, anyway. That'll give me time to double back to Santa Fe with you all and then on down to old Mexico or someplace until you break the story. I may even come fly you back, if you haven't misbehaved too badly with that frigid chick in the back seat."

"Come on."

"Actually, seeing you go all over seventeen for that cold pussy sort of turned me off, Steve." Her eyes said it had sort of hurt her feelings, too.

"It's the wrong reason to leave."

"Maybe yes, maybe no."

"I hope you do come back for me."

"We'll see how she goes."

The Pinon omnirange station drifted by below us, like a white clown hat on the harsh brown land. Pam turned north and pulled back the prop rpms, so that we made a fast descent to six thousand, which put us within a few hundred feet of the surface. New Mexico hurried by, the desert-heated air kicking us around this close to the sand and shale. I hung on, barely. Sonya Van Deer endured the uncomfortable ride, hugging her chest with her arms, keeping her eyes closed against the future.

After half an hour flying due north, Pam turned us more to the northwest and began climbing a little with the terrain, which had begun to change from the dun color of sand to rich reds and oranges, the blood of the Sangre de Cristo Mountains, rusty and sharp sloped, which floated toward us from the north. Gradually the mesquite and sage shaded into stunted junipers and pines, cooler-looking in a land nearly molten beneath the summer sun. The view from the air made the country look easy, with roads threading through those vivid, hostile mesas and foothills only a few miles apart. But you knew, once cast out into that hot red shale and juniper jungle, you could circle eternally and find no sign of life. Someone must have walked on my grave about then, for I shivered against the vibration of the plane.

Santa Fe came into sight around its corner of the mountain, a town poured upon the land, a town like a huge browned pastry, the buildings hand formed and baked into rounded loaves of adobe and tile. Pam was talking to the tower, slowing the airplane as we drifted west of the city toward the field, and down to what we believed was a final landing together on the north-south runway. She parked by the fixed base operation and shut down the Cardinal. "I'll just get topped off and be on my way, folks." She wouldn't look at me; her spade-shaped face had lost some of its radiance and gone stony.

"If I knew what to say to keep you with me, I'd say it."

"I know that, Steve."

"I hope you do."

"I'll keep in touch."

"I owe you a bunch of money," I said.

"We can settle up at home."

"Better we do it now, Pam. You never know . . ."

"Yeah, you might find a game or something."

"Right." So, sadly as a man paying his undertaker, I gave her the rest of Horatio's money and enough of mine to make a thousand. Then we just looked at one another while Sonya Van Deer got down from the plane and strolled toward the terminal. "Pam," I began.

"Look, we've got a lot between us. Let's not spoil everything with talk right now. Getting laid doesn't mean we have to walk into the sunset together. Neither does nearly getting killed. For all we know we wouldn't want to anyway. I'm glad you looked me up, hon. Maybe you will again. Maybe I'll be there. And maybe I won't."

"You don't leave me anything to say, Pam. I want you to stay. I'm going to miss you when you're gone."

"I know, Steve. You better go now." We kissed. I got out my bag and walked away from her, deliberately, fighting her gravitation all the way, telling myself, This is what she wants, this is how she wants it. When I looked back she waved, then turned away, gave herself back to her airplane. Okay, we forced ourselves apart.

I didn't look back again. I didn't want to see the Cardinal rise into the sky without me, the wheels tuck up into the fuselage; the little machine had become dear to me, along with its pilot. So I caught up with Sonya and we walked together like soldiers to the big, brown adobe terminal and found a telephone where I could call Randy Jones, the old pal who was going to save us.

5

Randy didn't quite splutter when she recognized my voice, but she nearly did, so that I felt I might have been more of a surprise than she wanted. But she recovered nicely, saying, "Steve, where are you?"

"I'm in town. I, uh, wondered if I could take you up on your offer."

"Well, sure . . ." Not certain but willing. Or maybe not, I decided. Maybe she was just running a quick inventory of her beer supply, or whether to put on some more tortillas, or something friendly like that.

"Sonya Van Deer's with me."

"Sounds cozy."

"It's a long story. I'll tell you when we see you."

"I can hardly wait." She laughed then, and the clouds cleared from the call. "My place is quite a bit south of the city, so it'll be quicker if you get a cab into town . . . the Hotel La Fonda. I'll pick you up there."

"Thanks, Randy."

"*De nada*, Steve."

I put the phone back and sorted through my feelings about the call. Some hesitancy at first, slowly kindling into warmth, although the Van Deer thing put her off. But she was a lonely, ugly girl, who lived somewhere in this molten desert; of course she'd like to see old Steve Borg and her old friend Sonya. Ego always answers us that way. Besides, I have a bad tendency to think my first questioning swipe at a problem tends to overcomplicate, so that my second time around invariably simplifies. Sometimes it works; sometimes it doesn't.

We got a cab outside the tan adobe pastry of the terminal and told the driver, a drugged blond woman of about twenty-five, we wanted to go to La Fonda. She drove us the ten miles in silence, which Sonya Van Deer and I occasionally broke with things like, "Have you been to Randy's before?" and her shake of the head, and my, "But you've been friends for a while?" and her, "Not that close, but friends, yes," and my, "She said she lived south of the city," and on, cold and friendless; I badly missed my sweet Pam, now aloft somewhere over the southern desert, coming up on old Mexico, with no friendly hand on her thigh.

Santa Fe rose on either side of us in rounded mounds of windowed adobe, brown and fluid, as though it had rained on large bread loaves. The narrow streets opposed the automobile successfully, so that the punks you saw cruising cruised slowly and delivery trucks wedged themselves into narrow brown alleys. It looked like a town where there wasn't a hell of a lot to do unless you belonged to the set whose life-style supported the slick magazine of the city, or did art, or sold it, or knew someone who did. Santa Fe smelled like grass—but, no, a whole city can't smell like grass. Like a Mexican kitchen, like something, I couldn't tell what, you smell where that kind of food is cooking. And La Fonda, where the cab left us, pleased me with its rich Mexicanness, for, stepping into the hotel, with its painted, gilded woods, atrium-dining room, and stuccoed walls and tiles and adobe exterior was for all the world like stepping into a giant *piñata*.

"It's like a big *piñata*," I told Sonya.

"Wait till the children begin banging on it," she replied, giving me a slightly skewed smile. I thought, What is it, does she sleep during the afternoon? For she seemed to have revived.

We took a quick walk around the lobby and went outside. I had begun to feel so unpursued as to be careless—forgetting, as I perpetually did, the size and weight of what pursued us. Now and then I'd flinch into a cautious attitude and scan the unfamiliar mestizo faces, the honkies, the rare black, looking for—God knows, maybe some failure of eye contact, or some official-seeming reluctance to have eye contact fail—something, and found that life just flowed around us.

It took me a moment to recognize Randy. She'd always dressed for Miami, had always hulked in mainlandized mu-mus and other free-flowing garments large enough to shield the Goodyear airship. Out here she dressed as a western mama, Levied and booted and khaki shirted, a frightening sight, a cactus version of the White Queen, but kind of beautiful too. Not until she hallooed with "Hey, Steve. Sonya, hi," did I identify the big podner walking toward us as our hostess; and then I grinned for her and returned her greeting, and Sonya did too. Randy came on as so hearty and happy that you had to begin to feel your spirit lift.

"I'm glad to see you, old friend," I told her.

"Me too, Steve." A shadow seemed to glide across the heartiness, but I put it aside, thinking, You can't hide the ugly little daughter, no matter how rough and tough you dress.

She walked us a block farther into the labyrinthine downtown, to a beige Toyota Land Cruiser, the car with which the Japanese revenged themselves upon the British. I stowed my bag and, Sonya in back again, swung up into the bucket seat on the right. Randy lowered herself into the driver's seat gingerly, like a tenth-century French knight, and then hurried us away into the congealed pulse of Santa Fe's short but turgid rush hour.

"How come you two got together?" she asked when we were hurtling south through the city.

"We have a common enemy, Randy," Sonya said, her voice loaded with irony.

"We're on the lam, honey," I said.

"Meaning, you don't want to tell me?"

"I will by-um-bye. It's a long story. When we're safe, when they can't get at us . . ."

"They?" She raised her eyebrows comically. "They?"

"They. And a big fucking *they* they are. A pair of large theys. Right now's the first time in human memory I haven't felt some killer bureaucrat just two steps behind me."

"I hope you're not bringing me into anything, man."

"I don't think I am. We covered our tracks pretty well. I don't think anybody knows we're here except you. By this time tomorrow I'll have filed my story, and they'll have to stop hunting us. So it shouldn't be a problem."

"I'm dying to know what's going on."

"Well said. Later, I'll tell you. But for now, let me enjoy being among friends for a change."

Randy gave me a sidewise glance that said she didn't like to wait. Or at least that's what I thought it said.

"How have you been, Randy?" Sonya put in, resisting the silence she felt closing around us, like meat-eating petals.

"Oh, you know. I'm always fine." Again, the shadow drifted over her. "The more things change, the more they stay the same."

"Let me see," I said, "In French that would be . . ."

We headed south on the interstate that curls around the southern foot of the Sangre de Cristos but turned off to the east soon after, leaving pavement and civilization behind. The Toyota scrambled up the narrow, badly rutted dirt road, pursued by a great beige dust cloud. We hung on and were carried into what, to a city boy like me, was wilderness. Intellectually I knew that a couple of miles, maybe four or five miles, back, ran a four-lane interstate and that Santa Fe was somewhere to the north. But out here there was nothing but the scrub junipers and livid blends of shale and rock and something mean in the prettiness of the land. The ride was disorienting, for we seemed to follow a ridge line for a while and I thought we switched back over it a couple of times. The sun still bumped along the western horizon, so I could tell my compass points; but it doesn't do much good to know you're somewhere east of the sun in northern New Mexico.

Finally the ordeal by Toyota ended.

We stopped inside an adobe wall, our dust cloud settling around us in the late sun, in a kind of diorama of the American nineteenth century. For Randy lived in one of those time machine homes you see here and there in the Southwest, a home of pale adobe and tile and old, gray timbers and stones and a courtyard with an arched adobe entrance holding a small bell. A pair of palominos danced in a corral out back. "Jesus, Randy," I said, "this is *fan*tastic."

A small Mexican woman with the old scar of a badly sewn harelip twisting her mouth slippered out to meet us, followed within leaping distance by a male Doberman who looked at me the way poor Marcia's boyfriend had, the dog no doubt checking to see if any prisoners were caught on barbed wire. "Hi, Uncle Ben," Randy told the animal. "Friends," she said, and you could tell the dog understood he wasn't to tear us apart at that moment. I hoped she'd keep reminding him. "Adelita, we have company."

"Yes, ma'am," said Adelita. I felt that one phrase might be all of her English.

"This is Mr. Borg and Dr. Van Deer, Adelita." We murmured hellos. She made us a grotesque little curtsey and yes-ma'amed twice.

We entered a large, tile-floored room, dark with wood and stonework and paintings; no sun followed us into the place, which felt so cool you wanted to drop down and put a hot cheek against the maroon tiles. In the middle of the structure an atrium opened to the sky, full of flowers that vibrated with color, even in the late-afternoon shadows. Birds kept dropping into the place for a drink, a bug, a bath, then flying away. "I'm surprised you get any work done," I told Randy.

"I put on a hair shirt."

"That explains it." We all laughed.

"Lots of room back here," she said. "I'm putting you and Sonya in adjoining rooms in back, so I won't bother you, and vice versa." Ha ha, we all said. She took us across the atrium and through a set of heavy french doors to another hallway and into one of two identical bedrooms that shared a bath back in the greater stillness and shadows of this part of the house. "One room has a sofabed; the other has a double. You guys can decide. If you want to wash up, I'll wait for you in the living room."

"I'll get my bag," I said, forgetting Sonya.

But she said, "I'm sorry to say I arrived without baggage, Randy."

"Not to worry. I keep spare toothbrushes and things like that around. I may even have a bathrobe you can wear, if you aren't too fussy about the fit."

So everything was fine. I went to get my bag out of the Toyota, skirting the immovable Uncle Ben, who eyed me insanely, wondering what to do. "Friend," I told him.

Sure you are, his wild, unblinking eyes replied.

6

By the time we got back to the living room, Randy had slipped into something tent sized but softer, become a linen mountain of hibiscus and fern, and was on the telephone in the corner where the stuccoed adobe fireplace oozed out of the wall. She'd lit a fire, a small one, to fight the faint chill that visits any desert after sunset. Hearing us enter, she put the telephone down, then turned to receive us like a real honest-to-Christ hostess, in her real honest-to-Christ beautiful desert home. I hadn't got used to the size and beauty of the place at all, wondered a little how she supported the estate, decided there was unearned income someplace, maybe from the missing father whose love—whose lost love—sometimes flickered as regret in her large, ugly face. "Hi, come in," she said, seeming to enjoy her role.

"I can't get over your place, Randy," I said.

"It's beautiful," purred Sonya, who had begun to remind me of a cat, sometimes giving, often cold, pretty, unsentimental; my interest in her braid had waned, and I missed my Pam, worried about her although she could handle herself a hell of a lot better than the rest of us.

Adelita shuffled into the room with a tray of big margaritas, and we each took one. Randy held hers up in a toast and said, "To our company. I'm tickled to death you guys are here."

"And to our hostess," I countertoasted. "An island of friendship in an enemy sea."

A frown touched her, then fled. "Nice of you to say."

"Nice of you to take us in."

"Mr. Borg, you need to tell Randy why we've come here," Sonya said, suddenly involved.

"Please, no nagging. But you're right. Want to hear, Randy?"

"I was hoping you wouldn't save it for bedtime."

"Come on. But there are problems, telling you this. When you hear about my situation, you're a target, like the others. I don't have to bring you in."

"Let me hear it anyway." Something cold in her voice? I couldn't say for sure.

So I told her, beginning at the beginning, which was the day of the conference out on Virginia Key, the day Vlad Danilov had died; I told her about Cerf and Dunham, that Chester was a murdering spook, told her about all the killing, the Huntsville Group, about *Brideshead, Kiev Centre,* and *Godfoot.* Everything, right down to our chat with Cerf that afternoon at Alamo Peak, everything in detail, really doing my first draft in my head, but also responding to an opportunity to tell the story to a friend; it had the appeal of talking over my adultery with Hester Prynne. "They're mopping up behind their mistakes, Randy," I finished. "Both sides are. That's why we're hiding now."

"And you're bringing them down on me."

"Look, I wouldn't have come if I thought they'd find me right away." Her eyes were all skepticism. "This time tomorrow I'll have filed my story with the *Herald.* Thirty-six hours, Randy, and then the story'll be out. There's no point in killing somebody to silence them when the story's out. We need a couple of days. Then it'll be over."

"If you say so." But then she added, "But, sure, you can stay a few days. I think you're right. In a couple of days they'll stop trying to silence you." I would think about that one later.

I sipped the margarita, which tasted something like tree bark, thinking how they probably made them bitter down here in the desert, with different tequila, thinking how we'd have one or two of these and eat dinner, and then it'd be time to get to work with the Adler portable, write the piece tonight, edit in the morning, file it by noon through the paper in Santa Fe. Randy seemed to read my thoughts, for she asked, "How far along are you on the story, Steve?"

"It's more or less written in my head," I told her. But Randy wrote for her living too. She knew there was some distance between the head and the hand, that this wouldn't be an easy story to get right. She just nodded, though, and the evening slid on. We talked, with the center of our discussion held by our large problems, by the story still to be written, by the death and disaster that had trailed us to her house; and yet, looking back, I can see that we handled all of these elements tangentially, talking them up but not out, moving around them, devouring time and intelligence in a kind of focused small talk. If you do any writing, you know that talking your subject to death in amiable conversation makes it damned hard to write about it later on. I knew it, but being able to talk about our situation in neutral . . . no, in friendly . . . company was irresistible. Anyway, we talked that way until Adelita came in and announced in Spanish that dinner had arrived. Randy led us into the dining room, a large stuccoed and tiled chamber full of iron candelabra and a giant-sized table of some dark wood and chairs you could swing your legs from if you were under six feet tall. Everything in the place was on Randy's scale.

And, God, the dinner was delicious. Adelita served up some tangy split-pea soup, guacamole (why isn't the avacado on the Mexican flag?), and enchiladas of the soupy type you get in the Indian-flavored Mexican food around the Sangre de Cristos. A little farther north and the enchiladas have congealed into the orderly cylinders you get at the border and from the franchised foodmongers. Even Sonya, cold cat that she was, dug in with gusto. Randy, enormous and out of control as her appetite for food may have been, professed a diet and ate around the corners of the meal, merely sipped at the riesling, and seemed to watch us, watch me especially, with a kind of motherly regret. I'd felt that from her before; my sleepy guard, startled awake, peered around like a doped dog and returned to sleep. We were safe here. I *knew* we were safe here.

"For dessert," Randy announced finally, "there's something special from my very own hand." We laughed appreciatively. "I really am dieting, and so I'm just going to watch. But you'll really depress me if you don't like this." Whereupon, Adelita entered bearing two bowls of chocolate mousse. "They're mousse with some cognac and whatnot mixed in. I've been known to make one big one and live off it for a day."

I wanted it to be superb, and it very nearly was. You dug down through the chocolate and encountered shades of cognac, or perhaps another liqueur, tastes wrapped in tastes, and these were fine; but there were also these shards of something sharp waiting for you in the sweetness. "It's very good," I told her.

"Yes, very," Sonya said, her lovely mouth pursed around the pudding.

"Thanks," Randy said.

"I don't know when food's tasted so good," I said.

"Thank Adelita for that."

"In Scandinavia they have a custom I sometimes miss," Sonya put in, suddenly inclined to speak, the cat coming round for a scratch. "At the end of the meal the guest makes a toast to his benefactors. Like this." She paused, like a poet about to recite a half-forgotten poem. Then, "Tonight I have arrived in a strange way, with a stranger, at the home of my friend, where I have enjoyed the intellects of my companions tremendously and where the food was as enjoyable as the discourse." She held up her wineglass as she finished and we all joined the toast and applauded afterward. Christ, I hadn't been so comfortable in what now seemed years as on that fine early evening south of Santa Fe. Maybe I felt we'd come close to the end of the trail, that our time as prey had become finite instead of open-ended. But I felt good.

I felt good through the after-dinner brandy and all the way to my room, saying fond goodnights to Randy, Adelita, the less-menacing presence of Uncle Ben, and Sonya, in whose braid I revived some interest. I said goodnight to all and went to my room, the one with the sofabed, and splashed water on my face and got out the Adler and some notes and sat at the little table there, wondering what the hell to write, wondering why I had come to this . . . But I felt good. Highlights caromed and zinged from the typewriter. Such notes as I'd typed out earlier crawled over *Herald* notepaper, the white shimmering, walking away . . . I splashed some more water on my eyes, thinking, Shit, the desert's made me blind, wanting to giggle at the roar of water pouring from the tap, tugged at by the whirlpool where it drained . . .

"But, *soft*," I whispered comically, teetering over the sink. "*Soft*."

My clothes fell away from my gleaming body like a shift. I turned the huge, glowing knob that opened the mirror to the room of the braid, walked elephant-wise into that darkness, and knelt by the side of the good doctor's bed. "Sonya," I whispered. "I've come to undo your braid." I giggled. She giggled back, turning under her sheet so that breasts appeared, rosy, golden, neon breasts trembling over sheets, and then the rest of her shimmering body, pubic hair like elephant grass (ho ho), strands of gold. I leaned past all this goodness for the moment and, with thumbed hands, unwove her braid, unwove it with the greed and wantonness of Rumpelstiltskin dealing in gold, for she shone, and over us the sky had begun to roar and cough and tremble; and then we came together in as many ways as we could, hot and mindless. If, before they tie me to the pole and shoot me, I should want a glowing sexual thought, I would think of this time with Sonya Van Deer.

We screwed and kissed and bucked and thumped for what seemed an eternity, for an hour or two anyway; and then, my thirst driving me away, I stepped into the cool tiled hall, naked, feeling like Quetzalcoatl, and made for where I believed the kitchen lay. Everything that entered my field of view came suddenly alive, gold-rimmed, silvered, gleaming, and there was that internal roar of the sky, plangent as a sea. And even this far nothing troubled me. If I thought, I thought, Too much brandy, or too much margarita, or too much wine. Nothing troubled me. So, silently, I made my way to the kitchen, for water, for a beer; who knew what the nude Borg would want, once there? Oh, God, I *did* feel good. I felt great . . . until I heard the low voices from the living room.

"Don't worry," the female voice said. "They'll sleep well tonight. They'll be here in the morning. Don't worry."

"I do worry. We had them before. I do worry," worried the male voice.

"John, they're on a fucking *peyote* trip. They're on it all night. Don't worry. Enjoy your drink. Then we'll find you an enchilada or something."

"A peyote trip?" asked the male voice, rhetorically.

"You sound like a narc." Female voice cackled in a laugh. "It just sharpens certain things. Makes life worth living."

"I guess it just seemed extreme." Subdued male voice.

While I listened my brain, my sorely peyoteed brain that perceived everything as wave motion and gleaming back lights and roaring heavens, tried to extricate me from the shit in which we had definitely settled. Who is John? it asked itself. Remember John, know any Johns, my man? My head shook itself, causing the room to go trapezoidal and collapse in the darker corners. "Everything seems extreme to you," said female voice. "I'm surprised they keep you on."

"Why're you on this ball-cutting binge tonight, anyway?"

"Sorry. No ball-cutting intended. Of course, you'd be the last place I'd look, Johnny."

"Jesus, locked in this bloody desert with a ball-cutting female. Jesus."

"Don't get angry." Female laughter. She must be a little drunk.

"Look, you're just getting squeamish, that's all. You haven't had to do a hell of a lot, just sit on your fat can out here and take our money to run your fucking *finca*. You didn't have to quiet old Wellman in Huntsville, for instance." Male voice brayed out the town's name, and I thought, still feeling fine, Sum *bitch*, John Chester.

"I'm not squeamish," female voice protested.

"The hell you're not. I remember how you handled the Miami thing."

"I handled it." Female voice went quiet, though. "I handled it," she repeated.

"Bullshit. You sprayed a room and even got the wrong person. I've always known you couldn't tell men from women, Chickie, but really . . . ?" He laughed at her.

"Enough, John."

"You like Borg. You like Van Deer. They're part of the world you'd like to blow, or lick, or whatever it is you do."

"Come off it, John. You're the blower. Let's keep our nomenclature pure." She rallied against him.

"We're going off track. The fact is, they want it quieted down. So far we've contained *Godfoot* pretty well. But they don't want any leakage on this one, nothing in the press about it, no matter what the breakage." They? They?

"That Huntsville thing went a little far, blowing everyone up. Like a bunch of anarchists."

"We didn't do that. Maybe it *was* old ammunition going off."

"Borg says the other side's cleaning it up too," she said.

"Who knows? We may wind up like so many gingham dogs and calico cats out in the desert."

Female chuckle.

"Friends, Randy?"

"Friends."

John Chester, I thought, suppressing a laugh. And Randy. No laugh to suppress. Chester had arrived to slay Quetzalcoatl, the braid, the young knight who undid it. Arrived in a NASA Lear jet no doubt, white charger, blue trim. Randy had called Chester in for the kill. No laugh? Nope. Tears grew around the boundaries of my wonderful gold-rimmed vision. She fed us full of peyote and now our heads are all fucked up, and in the morning they'll kill us and go after Pam, and everything would be tidied up . . .

I slithered back to Sonya's room, found her on her back fingering the golden swamp below her navel. "Sonya," I called. "Sonya, we've gotta split." She giggled. "Really. John Chester's here."

"John Chester?"

"He's come . . . to kill us." More laughter. "But, really, Sonya, he has. Randy's on their side." She shook her head, frowning, not quite able to catch hold. "We've got to get out of here."

"But I . . . I feel . . ."

"We're full of peyote. The dinner. The mousse. But we have to run." Smiling like a priest, she rolled out of bed and pulled her clothes over her wonderful metal and mother-of-pearl body, shiny as a robot in the starlight that washed our rooms. And I threw on my clothes, concealing my own gleaming body, stuffed my story notes into the windbreaker pocket, jammed the Magnum into my pants, and went back to her room, where she stood like a glass statue. "Come on," I said, and led her through the brilliant bursts of flowers in the atrium, where hoses coiled like mating pythons, plants sucked audibly at the roaring atmosphere, thrashed gently—vivid carnivores hunting through the vegetable night. Then we were out behind the house, the brilliant desert sky crashing and roaring overhead, the stars darting at us, stars of incredible magnitude, so that their light came to us early as a force, with weight, mass . . .

We hurried around a corner of the main building, into more pools of starlight, the red and gold land trembling under the night. There was no key in the Toyota, so we turned toward the gate, beginning to run as the peyote, which amplified everything else, began to amplify our fear.

The scratch of toenails in the shale behind us could have been a giant rodent. Turning, I found Uncle Ben loping out of the shadows, black and satanish, the irresistible archetype of dumb force, dog as machine. I hauled out the Magnum and brought it up in time to fire into the gaping mouth of the animal; and, it seemed very slowly, amid sound that enfolded me, that went right to my core with its reverberations, the vicious head exploded, showering its little crazy brain across the courtyard. We were gone before Uncle Ben hit the ground, running through the peyoteed landscape, moonscape, running without knowing where we ran to, unable to tell quite how the land lay, only that it rolled and gathered and unfolded in surreal waves, with every rock and bush radiantly outlined.

We ran till we could run no longer, until we collapsed against some titian rocks that vibrated with cruel noises, harmonizing against the sky. We could see no city lights, or even the lights of a neighboring house. The world lay in darkness that crackled and creaked and popped like a breaking shell. Looking at the sky I thought I could see a tear in it, and a huge horn-colored beak poking inward with the light.

For a time after we could move we chose to huddle in that rocky nest, like lost children in a forest. But then we heard them through the dope noises and night sounds—we heard the steps of their horses, the creak of tackle, muted by distance, and now and then a voice, Randy's or John Chester's. They revived our fear, drove us out of hiding, made us run blindly and doped and ill-prepared farther into the desert night.

7

Dawn found us dehydrated and dead with flight. We had stopped our plunge through the junipers and high-country brush, sore from running, badly scratched, our brains beginning to lose their zoom, so that the world that hurt us, dragged at us, threw great gold-rimmed rocks across our path, roared, became more real. With the light washing in from the east, light that looked more like normal illumination than the kaleidoscopic lights of our night, we could get an improved idea of where we had fled—or, rather, where we had been herded.

I remember a powerful account of prey, in which the writer described a huge wave of herring fry in shoal waters, pushed there by the presence of mackerel, who were held in place by a school of porpoises to seaward, all gathered there in the course of feeding, all held there by one another and by the greatest herdsman of them all: a large bull killer whale, whose sail cruised back and forth across the mouth of the bay, blocking the pathway to the open sea and freedom.

We had stumbled onto a long, flat ridge that curved a mile on either side of us into a crumbling slope that went nowhere. Its eastern slope ran sheer down to a tiny town, as small as it would seem from an airplane. And we were caught upon this ridge, between the crumbled ends, against the sharp drop into the valley. The horses' sounds had herded us up the hill, onto the ridge; Randy really knew the territory. From where we waited, at bay in a small pile of tangerine rocks, we could see the two riders, moving gently as that killer whale across our only exit, approaching slowly, letting the sun work on our thirst, the mild peyote hangover string out our fears.

Sonya had been silent for hours, exhausted, her face gaunt against the pale blanket of her upbraided hair. She cleaved to me now, and I to her; we kept touching to prove we lived, to prove we might survive. I had the Magnum out, watched the approaching riders over its barrel, wondering how close I dared let them come before I tried to pop Chester. Randy . . . I still didn't think she could kill us.

They took their time. The sun boiled up over the ridge, and still they rode along the middle distance, tiny figures that trembled in the heat that had begun to rise from the sunlit desert. The night's chill left us in the incredible brightness of the high desert, the sun an exploding star against a deep blue sky, the land an unrelieved wash of blood colors that burned into our brains. To Sonya I said, "I'm sorry I got you into this."

"You didn't, Mr. Borg. I did."

"Mr. Borg?" I smiled for her. "*Mr.* Borg?"

"Steven." She smiled back.

"I thank you for last night."

"And I you."

"If we get away, let's try it again."

"If we get away." Her voice caved inward around returning fear. And I went silent too, unable to think beyond that single enormous *If.*

"Steve?" Randy called from the distance, her voice faint and girlish in this silent, sound-devouring wilderness. "Steve, you can't go anywhere. We can deal. Come out. Throw out your gun. We can negotiate this."

"Bullshit," I murmured.

"She might," Sonya said, the cat clinging to some passing, pragmatic hope.

"All they want is to kill off their witnesses. That's *all* they want." I got up in a crouch and urged her to follow. "Come on," I said. We backed away from our rocks to the rim of the cliff and took up another, more desperate position there that gave us more cover to our front and protected our backs with empty space.

From this point, we watched them slowly close on us, walking their horses now until they were just outside the effective range of a poor shot with a big pistol, where they dismounted, both carrying M–16s. "Shit," I moaned. "Those goddamned guns." I'd seen trees cut down with those things. And civilians. Chester's saddle had a shovel strapped to it.

"Steve, Sonya," Randy crooned toward us. "We don't want to just blow you guys away. We want to talk. We want to negotiate this. Steve, all the company wants is your silence. We can deal. We're *authorized* to deal."

I squeezed off a shot at Chester. It kicked up a ten-foot cloud of dirt about two feet to his right. "Not too good, Borg," he yelled, then sprayed our general area with his M–16, which showered us with rock and sand. "Think you're outgunned. Maybe you should deal."

"Fuck you," I yelled back, almost as angry as I was frightened. "*Fuck* you."

They backed off a little, to confer. Their voices floated, unjoined syllables, murmurings, to us; but we couldn't understand what they said. I watched Chester, mainly, believing he was the more dangerous of the two and looked around in vain for the troop of cavalry I knew wasn't going to get us out of this. Hell, these people *were* cavalry. And we were the fucking Indians. But I looked around anyway. Once, a small plane droned overhead, a Cardinal, I thought, although they all looked alike to me, and I thought, wish I were there. The tiny cruciform diminished to a dot, blended with the terrain as it flew along the mountain toward Santa Fe, letting down, the life of its people going on . . .

While we died on this goddamned cliff.

I returned to watching Chester, and for a moment I couldn't tell anything had happened, not even when I heard the sudden blop-blop-blop of the chopper when it rose suddenly from the valley behind us—not even when I heard the shot. Chester just seemed to be watching me back, a little fixedly. But he'd been nailed to the Earth. A spot expanded on his temple, the back of his head showered tiny specks, cartoonlike; he stared into the sun with the spot just beginning to bleed down his 1950 vintage face, onto his fifties shirt, and then he dropped inaudibly in the larger silence of the desert. And even while I fastened on his death, tried to make an opportunity of the event without thinking much about its cause, I heard in the motor roar and wind the voice of a metallic man, saying, "Throw out your gun, Mr. Borg. We can easily pick you off. Both of you."

"Throw it down," Sonya panted.

I turned to look at Cerf, who balanced in the open doorway of a blue-and-white civilian Huey hovering fifty yards off our cliff. He held a scoped rifle in his left hand, with the sling wound around that arm, and hefted a bullhorn in the other. He looked like the guy who plays the harmonica and bass drum at the same time. And I knew he could pick us off as easily as he had John Chester. I could blaze away at the chopper and do nothing but kill some innocent bystander in a town a mile away; whereas Cerf could put one of those little red holes in my temple, in Sonya's. And would. I thought: He will anyway. But I couldn't throw away all our time, so persistent are one's dreams of rescuing cavalry. I thought about all those people who get murdered in their homes, waiting quietly for more and more time, and thought how easy it had been to join them. I tossed the Magnum out into the sand and stood up, my knees not very strong. Sonya balked and had to be raised.

And there, as the chopper circled, tail high and awkward, for its landing and kicked up storms of dust around us, and Randy strode toward us with her M–16 looking into our hearts, and Chester bled into the bloodish shale, we stood like two people in a play about the end of the world, pausing while the props got moved around; and our great flat ridge seemed to me the very rim of Earth.

The chopper touched, rocked gently, and settled while the rotor wound down. I looked at the pilot, anonymous, not thirty, male, Caucasian, not too interested in what his passenger did or to whom. You see that kind of destructive, disinterested neutrality in a lot of pilots' faces. Cerf stepped out of the craft carrying his sniper rifle, the sling still wound about one arm so that he could bring it up and put a couple of rounds into a gnat a hundred yards away. He wore his blazer costume and a blue-striped shirt, the collar crumpled around the narrow, schoolish tie, skewed today as always; and his bear face wore its dangerous grin. "I knew you didn't have very long, Mr. Borg," he said, "but this is ridiculous," and laughed raucously, flashing his metal teeth. He poked at Chester's body with one foot, rolled it over so we could share the sight of a bloody head stuffed with dark sand. "I'm getting better," he told Randy, who had walked over to him, who put her arm through the one he had wrapped in the rifle's leather sling. Affection in the desert.

"How are you, Andre?" she said and kissed him on his stony cheek.

"I can't complain, baby. We're very pleased with you, of course."

"Thanks." Ah, how she liked Cerf. Something extra warm shot through her when she had him around; he touched that deep chord in this big, ugly woman. Maybe he thought her beautiful. "I'd begun to wonder if you'd arrive in time?"

"In time?" He lifted his eyebrows; then, as though suddenly noticing us after a short loss of memory, he said, "Oh, you mean. . . ?"

Randy nodded.

"Well, Chester didn't seem to be handling things very well. Mr. Borg," he went on, projecting his rough voice toward me, "here is a cultural note for you. I find the quality of American agents is deteriorating. I also find they use their worst agents in scientific operations. What do you think of that?"

I didn't reply, saving my breath, for breath was life.

"Randy did not want to finish you off, Mr. Borg. Or you either, Sonya. She doesn't like killing. She's a wonderful shot, but she hates to kill. I don't know why she stays in the business."

He completed a gestalt for me: I remembered her talking to Chester about a "Miami thing" the night before and remembered Marcia's killer, a good shot gone nervous, firing wildly from the door.

"In Miami she did it for Chester, Mr. Borg. She can't live like a medieval Spanish lord on what we pay her, after all. But between your country and mine, we keep her in some style." He laughed harshly. "I don't believe she has ever killed for my side, although she would have today. You don't yet know that, Mr. Borg. She would have today."

"She just works for everybody," I said.

"You never cared much about sides, Steve," Randy responded, her tough voice holding a note of mild regret. Cerf was right. She would have killed us.

"You're right." Then, bluffing, I said, "The stuff I sent the *Herald* from Alamogordo is completely impartial. There are American clowns and Russian clowns. All kill."

"Last night you were still carrying the story in your head, Steve," she countered quietly. "Among other things."

"But the stuff the *Herald* got has the salient facts. If anything happens to me, to us, an editor'll put it together. My death would only improve my credibility."

"That depends entirely on the circumstances, Mr. Borg," Cerf put in, resuming control of the tableau. "You might simply disappear, for example. They're always finding bodies in shallow graves out here. An American pastime, is it not, Randy?"

"Sure it is." But he'd made her go grim.

Sonya revived enough to say, "But you owe *me* something," the feline instinct emphasizing the first-person singular. "I cooperated. I put the revised solar forecast into the system. It had its effect. Why do I have to die?" Her voice rose in a whine.

"You are such a weak-willed person, Sonya," he said as gently as he could. "You would fuck a pony and be photographed to save yourself. You would sell your young friend quickly. You would sell your father. . . ."

"I helped you because you threatened him."

"Old Andreev has always been a dying man, politically speaking. You knew that, you knew the risks he took. No, you worked for us because Vladimir Danilov asked you and applied a slight amount of romantic pressure to your weak will."

"Then certainly I'm too weak to do anything to you." Her voice was shrill. "Take him. You have him. But let me live. Why would you kill *me?*"

"For the company you keep, Sonya," Cerf said. "I'm sorry." The rifle jumped in his hand; she shrieked softly, torn away from me. I think she was dead before she sprawled a few feet closer to the cliff, her unbraided hair spread like wings across her shoulders. "You see, we mean business, Mr. Borg. In case you thought we didn't. Now. Go get that shovel off the saddle and dig Sonya a little grave while we talk." I did what he wanted, sucking away at such life as was left me, suddenly wanting every unpleasant second. And while I dug a narrow trench near Sonya's body, Cerf worked on me. "What we need, Mr. Borg, is to know exactly what it was you sent to your newspaper. We have all put so much into achieving silence on *Kiev Centre*, and your side has done all it can to contain *Godfoot*, I think you understand we are not easily deflected. We will not now have some third-rate reporter cancel our efforts. You can tell me what I want, or you can be forced to tell me what I want. So, tell me."

"Your efforts were canceled by *Brideshead*."

"That is beside the point. Tell me."

"I sent them what they'd need to write the story."

"What, the *Godfoot* story?"

"Our story and your story, Cerf." The words ate oxygen I needed, for the digging had begun to be hot work; the sun loomed overhead now, giving everything a wasted, dried-out shadow.

"Let's try again, Mr. Borg. What exactly did you send your newspaper? Tell me the number of pages, what was on each page."

I dug. Finally I said, "Ten pages, I think. Single spaced. First half on how I got to *Brideshead*. Then what's happened up to Alamogordo. Randy's right, I didn't get to finish it. But they have enough. A kid from a trade school could get a story out of what I sent." I went on itemizing, building an imaginary packet; it kept my mind off the work they had me doing. But gradually the shallow trench assumed a vaguely human shape. I kept digging, looking into the grave as though it were my tunnel out of there. "I sent pictures of Danilov's body," I told them. "We saw his body floating in *Excalibur*."

He cursed in Russian.

"I mean, Danilov is where this thing began," I said, finding it hard to breathe. "I was there at the beginning, wasn't I, Randy? Even before you gave them *Godfoot*?"

She nodded. Cerf, containing his anger, barked a sharp laugh.

"Chester had just recruited Danilov on that day, Mr. Borg. And Danilov had just recruited Randy."

"But he was double for a while," I said.

"Double, but with us, Mr. Borg. Always with us."

"At the end he regretted that."

"I know of his notes to you. He wanted you to understand so much, and you were so bloody slow about it. If he had returned from his *Kiev Centre* mission we would have had to take him in, rectify him, or . . . something. One can't simply say one will not help his mother country because it contaminates pure space. That is being silly."

"He still fucked you over, Cerf. You didn't get your results. And you can't contain the stories. They're on their way." Bluffing, bluffing, and tired to death, so that my resistance had to be punched up, like a feather pillow; the natural response to my troubles was to die.

"That's enough, Mr. Borg. Now put Sonya in and cover her. Perhaps I will say a few words."

I hesitated, sizing things up. I stood maybe twenty feet from the rim of the cliff, and they were maybe twenty feet away from me, standing a few feet apart; the chopper was another hundred feet away. Nothing you could fight with a shovel. I put the tool down and put my hands as gently as I could under Sonya's armpits, where the perspiration had already cooled. The skin was cold and ashen, and when I lifted her she had the limp, sandbag heaviness of all bodies that cannot help with the moving of them. I dragged her to my trench and lay her softly against the rocks and roots and unyielding bloody earth of the desert, smoothed her hair and brought it around to cover her face, thinking how, a few hours earlier, we had ploughed one another so thoroughly, in a false world the peyote had created for us. My eyes hurt and my throat constricted with the deadness of her; but no tears came, there was no water to feed the ducts. "Good-bye, Sonya," I whispered. "I'm sorry."

"So are we, Mr. Borg. Now, cover her up."

With the shovel I scraped the dirt back into the trench, gradually covering Sonya's body with the red and orange earth. When she had disappeared, when a mound rose over her, I gathered some rocks and piled them around the dirt, hoping to keep the animals off. I tinkered with the grave what seemed to me a long time, long seconds perhaps, long minutes maybe, eating time, stretching out my life, now it seemed so finite.

When I looked at Cerf again he gave the chopper pilot a signal, and the rotor began to wind up. "I think you are playing poker with us, Mr. Borg," he told me. "I can read your bluff in your eyes. Perhaps you sent enough to your newspaper and perhaps you did not. I think not. I think we are safe in ending your life here. Now you've seen how easily Sonya was disposed of. I want you to go peacefully as well." He advanced on me, ejecting cartridges from his rifle as he came, stooping to scoop up my Magnum pistol on the way. He nodded at Randy to cover us with her M–16, which she brought up at hip level and pointed at me, cold and steady as a fucking rock. "Look at her, Mr. Borg," Cerf said. "Does she look like a person who would not kill you?" Then he handed me the rifle. "There is one round in the chamber," he said.

I knew what he wanted. "You're asking me to kill myself."

He smiled. "A murder-suicide."

"It won't wash."

"We will make it wash, Mr. Borg. Remember that you tried to force your attentions on Dr. Van Deer in Miami. Obviously, you were strongly drawn. An autopsy will reveal your semen on her person. Please, go ahead with this so we can get out of here. It's uncomfortably hot." Although his face showed no moisture; he seemed to get rid of excess heat invisibly, like a furry animal.

I watched Randy, watched Cerf. Their eyes never flickered. I was lost in a land where serpents ruled. "If you want me dead, you've got to do it," I told them.

"Let me tell you the alternative, Mr. Borg. Randy is at least as strong as you are. I am perhaps twice as strong. If you don't do what we wish voluntarily, you can be made to do it involuntarily. We will simply push you through the motions, like a doll, and you still will have shot yourself."

I shuddered. Far away, another little plane, a dot, descended against a line of mountains. It made me yearn for Pam, for another chance to go on living; it made me glad she wasn't here, except they'd go after her now too and nail her . . .

"Go ahead, Mr. Borg. I tell you, if you do not, we will do it for you. How much humiliation do you want from this? It will happen. You can do it like a man. Or you can have your suicide performed for you, like a damned enema. What shall it be?"

I nodded but held up a hand for a little more time. "Let me . . . work on it, Cerf."

"Christ, you have nothing to stall us for, Mr. Borg. There is no help for you." He had to raise his voice over the whine of the chopper; we stood in its minor gale. The pilot chewed gum and watched us with that great neutrality, wondering only when he would once again begin to fly. Cerf spoke to Randy, too softly for me to hear, but she seemed to go more on the alert. He strolled to the chopper door. "Go *on,* Mr. Borg," he yelled.

The pieces had moved. I checked the board again. Here I was. Randy about twenty feet away. Cerf now well away, close to the chopper. I wondered how to use my single shot, maybe to nail Randy, perhaps to try at him . . . but he had the Magnum pistol dangling from one hand, and she had that goddamned M–16, which would tear me apart before I got the rifle sighted. But at least it wouldn't look like suicide.

"Please, Mr. Borg. We *will* have our way," he shouted.

"He's right, Steve," Randy said with something like compassion in her voice, but with none in her stony, ugly face. And I remembered how she'd talked to me in Miami, how she'd tried to warn me off, knowing that once in motion it would have to end with the killing of me.

Where was that little airplane, that dot? I felt the need to stall, to pray to some little dot, to speak to Pam about having her drift in and out of mind so intensely at the end. And then I saw it, the dot nearly at ground level a couple of miles beyond the tail rotor of the chopper, the dot so low it left a dusty wake, like a low-flying car. We couldn't hear the engine over the scream of the helicopter's turbine. I nodded for them and put the rifle muzzle against my jaw.

"Against your *temple,* Mr. Borg. Your *temple,*" yelled Cerf.

"Okay," I said, nodding. "Okay." The dot had the horizontal line of a high wing now. The Cardinal. Oh, God, the fucking cavalry! I looked around, wondering what Pam wanted me to do, wondering what her plan was. And then the Cardinal grew swiftly, flying not five feet off the desert, heading, not at the chopper, but a little to the right of it from where I stood . . .

I bit the dirt, and Randy brought up the machine gun to spray me when the lowered right wingtip of the Cardinal caught her between her shoulder blades, shattered her spine, and threw her a hundred feet; the large broken sack of her skipped off the lip of the cliff and fell eternally. The Cardinal yawed crazily, the low wing nearly digging in, then recovered, dropped over the cliff . . .

But I'd begun to move. I brought up Cerf's rifle, brought the sight up on the chest of the bear who, it seemed slowly, raised the Magnum in both hands toward me and squeezed off my single shot, feeling the rifle buck my shoulder and cheek. In the telescope picture, Cerf was flung backward into the chopper, his pistol discharging skyward. But I knew I hadn't killed him. I tossed away his rifle and scurried over to Chester's body, got his M–16 out of his stiff fingers, taking longer than I wanted, taking so long that Cerf reappeared in the doorway of the chopper, one arm hanging limp, the other bringing up the Magnum, and then the big pistol rounds kicking up towers of dust a few inches from my knees. But by then I had the M–16 up and talking, blowing sand and shale and holes in the chopper fuselage. Cerf merely stood in the doorway, trying to hit a distant, low-profile target with a pistol while he stood on a shifting platform that now began to lift into the air. It spoiled his aim, maybe his wound did too, and he emptied the pistol at me without hitting me and then stood there just clicking it at me. The pilot looked much less neutral now inside his big green headphones and continued his lift-off, Cerf clinging to the door with his good hand, huddled there against my barrage. As they sailed past the cliff I fired the rest of the magazine at that disinterested but frightened pilot. Glass flaked out of the greenhouse, and I lost my sight picture, but I stitched a line of slugs up across the turbine housing, which produced smoke and perhaps did something to the pitch control, or maybe the last burst got the pilot. The chopper rolled over to what aerobatic people call the knife edge, then rolled back; the nose pitched up insanely, the machine stalled, then fell off, slipping away down the valley. And all the while Cerf held himself in the doorway. Even at this distance I could see the grizzly eyes glaring at me, feel him radiating death. And then the disabled ship took him around a column of rock, out of sight.

I had been holding my breath.

Behind me, the Cardinal came in, tail very low, wheels extended like raptorial feet, the big flaps out, landing in the bloody wilderness. And, whatever had held me together through the hunt dissolved then. I went down on my knees and put my sorrowing head in my hands. If I'd been less broken I would have cried.

Epilogue

That's the story I wanted to tell. Not one about the *Excalibur* reentry so much as the large, destructive powers that wanted the reentry to produce for them, that wanted the deep indifference of space to yield a political harvest. You'll say, though, that this Borg is supposed to be a reporter, and yet there's been nothing about *Godfoot* or *Kiev Centre* in the press.

And I'll reply that I'm a reporter without witnesses.

Let me back up a little.

Pam sort of patted me back together and then sat there on the ridge where all that death had gone down, and we leaned together without speaking for a long time, out there in that deadly summer sun, in that blood-colored desert. After a while, believing a human voice would soothe me, she began talking, monotonically, bringing me back into her life. She said she'd lingered at Santa Fe to visit the flying museum, one of the few places in the world where you could still see an airworthy Grumman Wildcat, for example; and it had been near dark when she was ready to fly. But then the NASA Lear jet had landed and she'd seen Chester get out, so she decided to wait with the plane, uncertain how to help but willing to. She'd spent the night in the Cardinal and would have begun tracking us to Randy's place except that Cerf appeared at the airport with a chopper, made a telephone call, and scrambled. She followed, flying high, a shade slower than the Huey, and finally she'd seen our little tableau down on that ridge, which she called a mesa. She watched us as well as she could through her binoculars, but, "I couldn't tell what was going on really until I saw you digging and the lady stretched out on the dirt. Then I knew which side was which." She looked across the trembling bushes and sand at the mound of Sonya's shallow grave. "I feel bad about the competition."

"Me too," I said in a voice that barely worked. "Me too."

After some more holding and rocking, we stood up, rooted for a time in the desert, too laden with inertia to leave, knowing we had to. And then we got in the Cardinal, taking all the guns we could find with us, and she made a bumpy, marginal takeoff that floated us off the cliff below good flying speed, so that the airplane began to fly out over the valley. "Where to, hon?" she asked. I put my hand on her thigh, smiled, shook my head. "North," she said. "Let's go north."

So we flew up into Colorado, up the valley past Santa Fe and Taos, to Salida, and parked the airplane and went out into this new town in a car rented from the Ford dealership there and found an old motel off the major highway. And there, with a rented Royal manual and some paper and the notes in my jacket and my head, I wrote my stories, a series of four, covering our side, their side, the truth of *Brideshead*, and the bloody ending and double agentry of the last couple of days.

Pam took us down to Albuquerque where we put the manuscripts on Federal Express at the airport, along with a note to Terry Wilson saying I'd call him on some unspecified noon. But, even moving around in the plane, time expanded painfully, and we began to lean toward the approaching moment when our running would be over. So that I called Terry the next afternoon from El Paso. He'd read the manuscripts, he said, and was working on it. "But I've got to go to God on this one, Steve. Let me call you back." My neck hairs prickled. I told him I'd get back to him in about a day.

Away we went, to Dalhart, one of those little towns on the high plains where few trains stop and the airfield is small and old, its buildings driftwood gray, and the enemy has no ordinary approaches beyond the road going by the field. We spent a night together in which we were unable to touch, tense and grumpy with fear and, now, the sense that the end we had hoped for had moved once more out of reach.

When I called Wilson he said, "Bad news, Steve. They won't run the stories without a corroborating witness."

"Pam Rudd is with me. She's seen most of it." I spoke from the canoe of lost causes, though, and knew it.

"She's your lady. I mean," he added hastily, "I assume she's your lady."

"Bullshit, somebody told you she is. Terry, you're shitting me. This is an important goddamned story that's got to be told. You're letting them have me."

"Steve, we really looked hard at this one. We really wanted it to be an okay story, for your sake. And we even go along, up to a point. But, Jesus, the *size* of the conspiracy. I mean, we need proof."

"There is a dead chopper somewhere in that valley."

"No, there isn't. We checked."

"There're bodies all over the top of that ridge."

"There's nothing, man."

"Where's Randy Jones, then?"

"Her maid said she's on travel."

"Where's John Chester?"

"He died in bed three days ago, his doctor says."

"I had film of Danilov in my camera. I left it at Randy's."

"The maid says not. But we had the sheriff take a look anyway. Nothing, Steve. Just nothing."

"Jesus fucking Christ." The prayer of the lost.

"Steve, I personally think they won't hurt you, man. I don't know how it got to this, but I don't think they want to hurt you . . ."

I hung up. "Pam," I said through a throat that wanted to cry, "we gotta run."

She looked up, weary but not ground down. "They're not using your stories?"

"They don't believe me."

"Would they believe me?"

"They think you're mine."

"And so I am, hon. So I am."

Through the whole thing, I always believed that if I could illuminate the conspiracy, the evil in this fragment of government science, ours, theirs, I always believed if I could do that, they'd have to leave us alone. But they've destroyed every trace of the story beyond what Pam and I carry in our heads. They've got to the papers, to the magazines, so I've done the story in this form. Maybe some paper, some ballsy newscaster, will see it and believe it and help me drown my big enemy in light.

But, you ask, Why should *I* believe you?

It used to seem an easy question to answer. Now I can't answer it at all. I don't know. I think, maybe, listening to me, hearing a sane tone running through my narrative, you'll believe it happened. I count on that.

Let me tell you how things are with us now. I can't say where we are. It is primitive, strangers are easily detected, as we were when we first came here. The Cardinal is gone, replaced with another machine with which Pam gets part of her living; the rest comes from the sale of her Ruddy Good Flying equipment, although it surprised me how little of it she owned outright. I do some writing, freelancing under other names, in other styles. We live on a hill, the house sheltered among rocks and trees—whether firs or palms, granite or shale or limestone, I won't say—with an excellent field of fire. The M–16s and Cerf's rifle are never far away. They've trained us to kill, like riflemen turned from children into people who shoot other people; our life is like a combat patrol through a jungle. That is how we go along now.

We've left them a very cold trail. Only once since I began to tell my story in this form have we seen a stranger we were pretty sure had come hunting us, a stocky blond man in a tweed sportscoat and flannel pants, furtive and obvious. We stalked him for a time and would have put him away, except he left. Our visible trail ends a long way from here, out where we send forsaken mothers Christmas cards and birthday flowers, mail manuscripts, pick up such change as their sale brings in. Hunting here for us is work for gamblers, and we keep the stakes high. If *they* get close, we'll shut them down. If they make it too hot, we'll move on, hurrying out eight hundred or so miles and vanishing again. It makes a big circle, and we are consummate hiders now. Consummate prey.

But my ambition is to walk through a city with my fine English-looking woman, openly ourselves, openly bonded, able to be happy; to have no reflexive need to see who walks behind us, to check our doors for who disturbed our alarms of spiderwebs and hairs, none of those recently discovered reflexes, no fear of a golden-toothed man who walks like a bear.

I hope you believe me. I hope you will help.